## 'Hi! That was good timing.'

Tom came over to join them, stooping down so he could say hello to Charlie, who responded by holding up his arms to be picked up. Tom laughed as he lifted him out of the pram. 'Tired of being strapped in, are you, Tiger? I don't blame you.'

He balanced the baby on his hip, making it look so natural that Hannah couldn't stop her previous thought resurfacing. Tom would make a wonderful father—a father who would love and care for his child no matter what. A lump came to her throat and she cleared it, afraid that her emotions would get the better of her.

'He hates being fastened in for long, which doesn't bode well for the evening. I only hope he doesn't disturb everyone when they're trying to enjoy their meal.'

'Nobody will mind,' Tom assured her. His eyes skimmed over her and he smiled. 'You look really lovely tonight, Hannah. That dress suits you.'

'Oh. Thank you.' She felt the heat rush up her face and turned away. *He probably says that to all the women,* she told herself bluntly, but it had little effect. Maybe he did dish out compliments readily enough, but there was no doubt that he had been sincere.

The thought was a boost to her ego. As she led the way into the pub she couldn't help thinking how *good* it felt to be appreciated.

**Dear Reader**

Single mums seem to get a lot of bad press these days, yet in my experience they do a fantastic job of raising their children under very difficult circumstances. My own mother became a single parent after my father died, and I know how hard she worked to give me a happy home life. My latest trilogy, *Bride's Bay Surgery*, focuses on three single mums, Hannah, Emily and Becky, who are committed to do their very best for their children.

In the first book of the series Hannah is determined that she will do all she can for her little boy. She doesn't have time for a relationship, so when she meets Tom Bradbury she is determined to keep him at arm's length. Tom is equally determined not to get involved. His family has a poor track record when it comes to love and marriage, so he has made up his mind to remain single. However, that was before he met Hannah. Meeting her makes him reassess his whole attitude to life!

I hope you enjoy reading Tom and Hannah's story as much as I enjoyed writing it. If you would like to contact me then please e-mail me at the following address: Jennifertaylor01@aol.com. I would love to hear from you.

Best wishes

*Jennifer*

# THE FAMILY
# WHO MADE HIM
# WHOLE

BY
JENNIFER TAYLOR

First published in Great Britain 2012
by Mills & Boon, an imprint of Harlequin (UK) Limited.
Large Print edition 2013
Harlequin (UK) Limited, Eton House,
18-24 Paradise Road, Richmond, Surrey TW9 1SR

© Jennifer Taylor 2012

ISBN: 978 0 263 23099 4

Harlequin (UK) policy is to use papers that are natural, renewable and recyclable products and made from wood grown in sustainable forests. The logging and manufacturing process conform to the legal environmental regulations of the country of origin.

Printed and bound in Great Britain
by CPI Antony Rowe, Chippenham, Wiltshire

**Jennifer Taylor** lives in the north-west of England, in a small village surrounded by some really beautiful countryside. She has written for several different Mills & Boon® series in the past, but it wasn't until she read her first Medical Romance™ that she truly found her niche. She was so captivated by these heart-warming stories that she set out to write them herself! When she's not writing, or doing research for her latest book, Jennifer's hobbies include reading, gardening, travel, and chatting to friends both on and off-line. She is always delighted to hear from readers, so do visit her website at www.jennifer-taylor.com

**Recent titles by the same author:**

GINA'S LITTLE SECRET
SMALL TOWN MARRIAGE MIRACLE
THE MIDWIFE'S CHRISTMAS MIRACLE
THE DOCTOR'S BABY BOMBSHELL*
THE GP'S MEANT-TO-BE BRIDE*
MARRYING THE RUNAWAY BRIDE*
THE SURGEON'S FATHERHOOD SURPRISE**

*Dalverston Weddings
**Brides of Penhally Bay

**These books are also available in eBook format from www.millsandboon.co.uk**

For Max, my gorgeous little grandson.
The best Christmas present I've ever had.

# CHAPTER ONE

'AND this is my godson, Tom Bradbury. Tom has very kindly been helping out until you arrived. Tom, this is Hannah Morris, my new colleague. I'm sure you must be almost as delighted to see her as I am!'

'Nice to meet you, Dr Bradbury.' Hannah pinned a polite smile to her lips when the younger man laughed. She wasn't going to be drawn into asking why he should be so pleased to see her because she wasn't interested. She'd had her fair share of tall, dark, handsome men and intended to steer well clear of anyone who fitted that description in the future.

'It's good to meet you too, Hannah. But, please, forget the title and call me Tom.' He held out his hand, leaving her with no option other than to take it.

Hannah felt a quiver of awareness run through her when their palms touched and tensed. She didn't want to feel anything for this man, yet there was no denying the surge of electricity that was racing along her veins. It was a relief when he released her and turned to Simon Harper, the senior partner in the practice.

'We don't stand on ceremony around here, do we, Simon?'

'Certainly not.' Simon smiled at her. 'Most of our patients call us by our first names, so I hope that won't bother you, my dear. The days when the local GP was considered only second to God in the pecking order are long gone, I'm pleased to say.'

'Of course not.' Hannah summoned another smile although she had to admit that the idea of being on such familiar terms with her patients would take some getting used to. She had always preferred to maintain a professional distance and hadn't encouraged that kind of familiarity, but if that was the way things were done at Bride's Bay Surgery then she would have to get used to it.

'I'd stop right there if I were you, Simon. You don't want to scare her off!'

Hannah stiffened when Tom Bradbury laughed again. He really did have the most attractive laugh, she thought, the richly mellow tones making goose-bumps break out all over her body. She cleared her throat, refusing to dwell on the reason why it'd had such a strange effect on her. 'There's no danger of that. Although, admittedly, I'm more used to my patients calling me Dr Morris, I'm sure I shall adapt.'

'That's the spirit.' Simon gave her an approving smile. 'I knew I was right to pick you for this post, Hannah. You're going to fit in *perfectly* around here.'

Hannah murmured something although she couldn't deny that Simon's unwitting choice of words had touched a nerve. She had always tried to be perfect in everything she did. Right from the time she had been a child, lining up her dolls in perfectly straight rows, she'd had a compulsion to make her life as flawless as possible. She knew what it stemmed from, of course. When she was seven her father had been involved in a serious road accident. She could still remember the horror of wondering if he would survive. The only way she'd been able to cope was by making everything else in her life as perfect as possible. To her mind, if everything was in its proper order then things would turn out right.

Thankfully, her father had recovered; however, the need for order had remained with her as she'd grown up. When she'd met Andrew, and discovered that he had felt the same, it had seemed as though they had been meant to be together. They could each strive for perfection, knowing the other would understand. It was only in this last year that she had realised what a terrible mistake she had made.

'Hannah?'

Someone touched her on the arm and she jumped, feeling the colour rush to her cheeks when she found Tom Bradbury staring down at her. At over six feet in height he was a lot taller than her and she was suddenly struck by the difference in their stature. He looked so big and solid as he stood there with a frown drawing his black brows together that she had the craziest urge to lean on him. The past twelve months had been hard and it would be wonderful if someone could take the burden off her for a little while…

'Are you all right?' He stepped closer, his blue eyes filled with concern as he peered into her face, and Hannah realised with a start that she had to pull herself together. Tom Bradbury wouldn't be interested in her problems, neither did she want him to be.

'I'm fine, thank you.' She looked around the room. 'Where's Simon?'

'He's gone through to the house to make some coffee, or, hopefully, he's gone to ask Ros to make it for us.' Tom smiled and she was relieved to see that his face held nothing more than the sort of polite interest one showed to a stranger. 'A word of advice here from one who knows: if Simon offers to make you a cup of coffee, refuse. His coffee is enough to make strong men weep!'

An unwilling smile curved Hannah's mouth. 'It can't be that bad, surely?'

'Oh, it is. Trust me.' Tom chuckled. 'Simon may be a brilliant doctor, adored by all his patients, but his coffee is in a league of its own. If you value your health then make sure you get to the kettle before him!'

His blue eyes held hers fast for a moment before he turned and headed towards the door and it was only then that Hannah realised she had stopped breathing. She took a quick breath and then a second for good measure before she followed him. It was the newness of it all, she assured herself as he led the way along the corridor towards the house. The fact that this was her first day in a new job, the first day of her new life, in fact. She was bound to feel on edge and keyed up....

He pushed open a door, waiting politely for her to precede him, and Hannah sucked in her breath when her shoulder brushed his chest as she passed. Maybe it was understandable that she should feel nervous when she had needed to make so many changes to her life of late, but did that really explain why her blood pressure had shot up several degrees and her pulse was racing?

She sighed as she stepped into an attractive country-style kitchen because she knew what the answer was even if she didn't like it. The reason her heart was racing and her blood pressure was soaring was standing right behind her. Tom Bradbury was to blame. He and he alone had made her feel all those things. Admittedly, it was a surprise to find herself responding this way, but she mustn't let it throw her. Maybe she *did* find him attractive but that was all it was—pure physical attraction, nothing more. After all, she had just escaped from one disastrous relationship and she certainly didn't intend to find herself caught up in another one!

Tom took the cup of coffee Ros offered him and walked over to the window. It was the middle of May and the sun was glinting off the sea. It was the kind of glorious Devon day that always made him glad to be alive but for some reason he was less aware of his surroundings at that moment than he was of the woman behind him.

He took a sip of his coffee and turned, letting his gaze rest on the figure seated at the table.

Hannah Morris was pretty in a restrained kind of way with that pale, fine skin and that rich auburn hair that fell softly to her shoulders. Her eyes were green, a deep sea green—he'd noticed that before—framed by thick black lashes that he would swear hadn't been enhanced by even a trace of mascara. In fact, now that he thought about it, she was wearing very little make-up, just a touch of gloss on her lips and maybe, although he couldn't be sure, a hint of blusher on her cheeks.

Tom took a larger swallow of his coffee, somewhat surprised that he had taken such an interest in Simon's new colleague. Although his godfather had told him about Hannah Morris when he had decided to offer her the job, Tom was aware that he hadn't really been listening. All he could recall was that she was thirty-one years old and had worked at a large practice on the outskirts of London for the past few years. What else Simon had divulged had gone in one ear and out of the other and all of a sudden he wished that he'd paid more attention. There was something about

Dr Morris that intrigued him, and it wasn't just the fact that it had been a long time since he'd reacted *that* strongly when he had touched a woman's hand!

The thought caused him more than a little discomfort so it was a relief when Ros appeared at his side. 'Penny for them.' She smiled up at him, her face breaking into the warmly caring smile that had made Tom wish on more than one occasion when he'd been growing up that she had been his mother instead of the more glamorous Tessa.

'I'm not sure they're worth a penny even with the current rate of inflation,' he observed dryly, then changed the subject. 'Glad to see you got to the coffee pot before Simon.'

'Oh, no fear of that. I had the coffee on the go by the time he appeared.' Ros laughed but he could tell that she wasn't fooled by his airy dismissal of her question. Ros knew him far too well, a fact he must bear in mind when his thoughts were tempted to wander again.

As though unable to resist, his gaze moved back to Hannah and he felt a shudder run through him when he discovered that she was watching him. Just for a moment their eyes met before she looked away but it was long enough. Tom took another gulp of coffee, hoping it would quell the tremor that had been triggered inside him, but no such luck. He could feel it working its way down his body and inwardly groaned.

He didn't do this kind of thing! He didn't respond so instantly to a woman, certainly never felt as though he had suddenly found himself with one foot on an emotional roller-coaster that was about to speed off. He liked women, enjoyed their company, but the key word in that statement was *women*.

He liked them in the plural. When he dated he always made it clear that he was happy for his date to see other men, as he would be seeing other women. However, he knew without the shadow of a doubt that Hannah Morris wasn't a plural type of woman. She would expect any man she dated to be strictly faithful and if there was one thing he couldn't guarantee it was that kind of commitment.

'So what do you think of Simon's new protégé?'

Tom dragged his thoughts back into line as he turned to Ros, although he had to admit that he was more than a little stunned by the way he was behaving. He had known Hannah Morris for less than ten minutes and yet here he was, pondering the weighty matter of his own shortcomings. 'She seems very nice.'

'Nice!' Ros hooted. 'Is that the best you can come up with, Tom? She's *nice*?'

'Well, I've hardly had a chance to get to know her,' he countered, a shade defensively.

'Maybe not, but it's not like you to be so slow.' Ros's eyes were filled with laughter as she looked at him. 'Usually, you have a woman summed up and categorised in less time than this.'

'Categorised? I'm not sure I know what you mean,' he said stiffly.

'Oh, come on! Of course you do. I've watched you growing up, don't forget. I've seen the effect you have on the female half of the population and watched you in action, too.' Ross chuckled. 'I'm not sure if you use some sort of scoring system but women seem to fall into one of two categories where you're concerned. They're either fair game or strictly off limits. What I can't work out is which category Hannah comes into.'

'So what are you two muttering about?' Simon came over to refill his cup and smiled at them. 'You look as though you're plotting some sort of mischief.'

'Mischief?' Ros took the cup off him. 'It's a long time since I could be accused of causing any mischief!'

Tom moved away while Ros topped up her husband's cup, relieved to have been let off the hook. He frowned as he turned to stare out of the window again. Was Ros right? Did he view women in such a calculating way? He hated to think that he did, yet he knew in his heart it was true.

Since his first—and only!—ill-fated foray into love, he had been determined not to leave behind a trail of destruction like his parents had done. Although he enjoyed dating, definitely enjoyed sex, he didn't do the rest and he never would. There would be no happily-ever-after for him.

No wife and family gathered around the hearth waiting for his return. He preferred his life to be free of such complications and that way nobody would get hurt, neither him nor some poor un-suspecting woman who'd had the misfortune to fall in love with him.

He glanced round when someone laughed, felt the hair on the back of his neck lift when he re-alised it was Hannah. In that second he knew that although he may have managed to avoid commit-ment in the past, he might find it harder to do so in the future. There was just something about Hannah Morris that drew him, something he could neither explain nor reason away. He could only thank his lucky stars that he was leaving. By this time next week, he would be on his way to Paris and he would make sure it was a long time before he came back!

Hannah spooned a little more sugar into her cup as she listened to the affectionate banter between Simon and his wife. It was obvious how fond they were of each other and she couldn't prevent the sudden pang of envy that rose up inside her. She had hoped that she and Andrew would have that kind of a relationship, but it hadn't happened. There had always been a certain distance between them even though they had appeared to have had so much in common. It was funny how you could think you knew someone and be proved so wrong.

'More coffee, my dear?'

Simon reached across the table for her cup but she shook her head. 'No, thank you.' She turned and smiled at Ros. 'It was delicious but I'll be buzzing if I have any more.'

'I know what you mean.' Ros smiled back. A pretty woman in her fifties with light brown hair that curled around her face, she exuded an air of calm that was very soothing. 'I have to limit myself to no more than three cups a day otherwise I'm high as a kite on all the caffeine!'

Hannah laughed when Ros pulled a rueful face. She glanced round when a movement caught her eye and felt herself tense when she realised that Tom Bradbury was watching her again. It had happened several times now; she had glanced up and found him staring at her and she wasn't sure what to make of it. Was it just the fact that she was new or was there something more behind his interest?

She hurriedly dismissed the thought, refusing to go down that route. She wasn't looking for romance. She just wanted to be left alone to create a new life for herself and her son. Charlie was all that mattered, his happiness was her main concern. Everything else was inconsequential.

'Simon told me that you have a little boy, Hannah. What's his name and how old is he?'

Hannah roused herself when Ros spoke. 'His name's Charlie and he's nine months old.'

'And into everything, I bet!' Ros laughed as she turned to her husband. 'Remember when our two were that age? You needed eyes in the back of your head. They're twins and that made it worse, of course, but I wouldn't have believed the havoc they could cause if I hadn't seen it for myself.'

Hannah smiled, trying not to let Ros see that the remark had hit a nerve. Sadly, Charlie couldn't get up to very much mischief. He had been born with talipes—club feet—and at the moment his legs were encased in casts, which severely restricted his movement. Although he was a happy, intelligent little boy, he wasn't able to do a lot of the things a child his age normally did. Still, she consoled herself, once the casts came off the situation should improve, and if they hadn't worked there was a good chance that a second operation would solve the problem.

'Do your children still live in Bride's Bay?' she asked, changing the subject because the thought of her son needing further surgery made her feel a little panicky.

'I wish!' Ros sighed. 'Daniel is a research botanist. He's in Borneo at the moment, tracking down a plant which the locals claim has healing powers. And Becky moved to New Zealand with her husband a couple of years ago. She's just had a baby, a little girl called Millie, and as you can imagine we're dying to see her.'

'We'll get over there as soon as we can,' Simon assured her, patting her hand.

'I know, darling, but I don't want to wait, that's the problem. Babies grow so quickly and I just feel that we're missing out on so much...' Ros stopped and gasped. 'Why didn't I think of it before! I mean, this would be the ideal time, wouldn't it? Tom knows the ins and outs of running the practice almost as well as you do, and now that Hannah is here, we're fully staffed.'

She turned beseechingly to Hannah. 'If you and Tom would hold the fort, it means that Simon and I can go and visit our first grandchild!'

# CHAPTER TWO

'PLEASE take a seat, Mrs Granger.'

Hannah waited while the woman made herself comfortable. It was almost lunchtime and Barbara Granger was her last patient. The morning had been surprisingly busy. She'd not had a minute to herself, in fact, and suddenly found herself wondering if she should have accepted Tom Bradbury's offer to split her list. It would have made far more sense to ease herself in gently, yet she'd felt strangely reluctant to accept his help. Something had warned her that once she did, it might be difficult to stop.

The thought was so ridiculous that she was hard pressed not to show her disgust. Tom Bradbury meant nothing to her. He was just someone she would be working with for a short while, although, if Ros had her way, it might be longer than either of them had anticipated. The idea was disquieting and she had to make a conscious effort not to dwell on it as she smiled at the woman seated across the desk.

'I'm Hannah Morris, the new doctor.'

'Nice to meet you, dear.' Barbara Granger smiled back. 'I'm sure you'll be very happy here. Bride's Bay is such a lovely little town—everyone is very friendly, as you'll soon discover. Margery worked here for over ten years and we were all very sorry when she decided to leave.'

'I'm sure she will be missed,' Hannah agreed. Every patient she had seen had commented on how sad they'd been when Simon's previous partner had left. It had made her realise what an integral part of the town the practice was. After working in London, where patients rarely formed a close attachment to their doctor, it was good to know that she was now a valued part of the community.

'Yes, she will. But folk have to do what's best for them, don't they.' Barbara settled her handbag on her knees. 'I know how much Margery missed her family. Her two sisters live in Edinburgh and it will be lovely for her to be able to spend more time with them.'

'It will indeed. Now, what was it you wanted to see me about, Mrs Granger?' Hannah gently steered the conversation back to the reason for the visit. 'Is something worrying you?'

'Yes, although it's not about me. It's my Peter, you see. He's going into hospital soon and he's in a right state about it.'

'Is Peter your husband?' Hannah asked gently, wondering about the ethics of discussing the matter. Patient confidentiality was a key issue and she wouldn't want to cross any boundaries.

'No, my son.' Barbara sighed. 'Peter has Down's syndrome. I should have explained that to you before I began.'

'It's quite all right,' Hannah assured her. 'I take it that you are his main carer?'

'I was until last year when he got a place in an assisted living facility in the centre of town.' Barbara pulled a face. 'Such a horrible name. Calling it a facility makes it sound like some sort of institution but it's nothing like that. The local council converted one of the houses near the post office so it could be used by people with disabilities like my Peter's, and it's very homely. He loves it there.'

'That sounds like a wonderful idea,' Hannah said enthusiastically. 'Your son has his independence, yet there are people around who can offer support if he needs it.'

'Exactly. Oh, I wasn't sure if he should go when Simon first suggested it. His dad left soon after Peter was born. He couldn't handle the thought of having a handicapped child, you see, so I've looked after Peter by myself. It's always been just the two of us and I was worried in case it was too much for him, but he's come on in leaps and bounds, as it turns out.'

'You must be so relieved,' Hannah agreed quietly. As the single mother of a child who needed extra care, she understood how difficult it must have been for Barbara. Maybe it was different when both parents were involved; at least they could discuss any issues and reach a decision together. However, it was much harder when you were solely responsible for your child's welfare, as she'd discovered.

She knew how she'd agonised over Charlie's treatment, spending many a sleepless night worrying about what it entailed. It would have helped enormously if she'd had someone to talk it over with but, like Barbara Granger, she'd been on her own. It must have taken a lot of courage to allow her son to leave home, Hannah thought admiringly as she smiled at her.

'So why is Peter going into hospital?'

'He needs an operation on one of the valves in his heart. As I'm sure you know, dear, a lot of people with Down's have heart problems, so it isn't the first time Peter has needed treatment. It was fine while he was a child—I was able to stay in the hospital with him. But now he's nineteen and classed as an adult that isn't possible. He's getting very anxious about it, which is why I thought I'd have a word with you.'

Hannah frowned. 'I understand your concerns, Mrs Granger, although I'm not sure what I can do to help. Can you leave it with me? I'll speak to Simon and see what he suggests.'

'Of course.' Barbara stood up. 'Just give me a call when you've worked something out or, better still, pop in for a coffee if you're passing. I live right next door to the nursery and you can always call in after you've dropped off your little boy. Lovely little chap. Let's hope they can sort out that problem with his feet, eh?'

Barbara bade her a cheery goodbye, obviously finding nothing unusual about the fact that she knew so much about Hannah's private life. Hannah shook her head as she gathered up the notes she had used. She had been in the town for just two days and already it seemed that everyone knew all about her!

'Was that Barbara Granger I saw leaving?'

Hannah jumped when a deep voice addressed her from the doorway. She looked up, trying to quell the racing of her heart when she saw Tom standing there. He had shed his jacket and rolled up the sleeves of his pale blue shirt so that his tanned forearms were bare. He looked so big and overwhelmingly male that her mouth went dry. She may not be in the market for another relationship but she would need to be dead from the neck up *and* down not to be aware of him! It was only when she saw one dark brow lift that she realised he was waiting for her to answer.

'It was. Apparently, her son is going into hospital soon and he's getting very stressed about it,' she said, shuffling the notes into a pile.

'Something to do with Peter's heart, I take it?' Tom came into the room and stopped beside the desk. Hannah continued her shuffling, although for some reason her normally deft fingers seemed to have all turned to thumbs.

'Mmm. He needs an operation to repair one of the valves.' The pile of notes suddenly disintegrated into an untidy heap and she clamped her lips together in annoyance. Picking up the top few folders, she tried again then jumped when a large hand appeared in front of her.

'Here, give me half and I'll help you carry them through to the office.'

Tom didn't wait for her to comply with his offer

as he scooped up half of the buff envelopes and Hannah had to bite down even harder to stem the retort that was trying to escape. She didn't need his help, but short of making a scene there was little she could do.

She trailed after him, aware that she was in danger of making a mountain out of the proverbial molehill. Tom was just trying to be helpful and it was stupid to see it as a threat. She knew it was true yet it was difficult to accept it. She really didn't want to be beholden to him for anything.

He plonked the notes into a tray then stood aside while she deposited hers on top. 'Lizzie will sort them out when she gets back from lunch,' he assured her, resting one lean hip against the edge of the desk.

'It might help if I put them into some kind of order,' Hannah murmured, taking a couple of folders off the pile.

'There's no need. Lizzie is a whiz with the filing. She'll have them sorted in no time.' He took the folders off her and dropped them back into the tray, leaving her gasping at his high-handedness.

However, he seemed oblivious as he returned the conversation to what they had been discussing.

'Peter is a lovely fellow. Although he has Down's, he's quite a high achiever. He works at The Ship Inn, collecting the empty glasses and, occasionally, waiting on in the dining room if it's busy.'

'Really!' Hannah exclaimed in surprise.

'Yes. That's the joy of a place like Bride's Bay. Folk look out for one another and do all they can to help. Mitch Johnson, who runs the pub, took Peter on last winter and it's worked out really well for everyone.'

'That's wonderful. I had no idea people were so supportive. Where I worked before, there were plans to build a unit for people with disabilities like Peter's but the local residents objected and it didn't go ahead.'

'Sadly, that happens all too often. I'd put it down to ignorance if I didn't have a nasty suspicion that it was more a fear of it having an impact on property prices than anything else.' Tom shrugged when she looked at him. 'If you live next to one of those units, you could find that the value of your home drops.'

'I'm sure you're right.' Hannah was surprised by how disgusted he sounded. She wouldn't have summed him up as someone with strong altruistic leanings, although why she should have made that assumption it was impossible to say. She hurried on, not wanting to dwell on the thought that she might have been unfair to him. 'Anyway, I was going to have a word with Simon to see what he could suggest. It sounds as though Peter needs some reassurance.'

'The hospital has just instigated a scheme whereby vulnerable adults are given a tour of the areas they'll be using during their stay.' Tom straightened and went over to the filing cabinet. 'They sent us a leaflet only last week if I can find it… Ah! Here it is.'

He handed her the leaflet and Hannah sucked in her breath when their hands brushed. She murmured her thanks as she took it over to the window to read, although for a few seconds the words seemed to dance before her eyes. She had to stop this nonsense, had to stop reacting whenever Tom touched her. It was ridiculous to be this responsive to a man she barely knew.

The thought steadied her. She skimmed through the leaflet and nodded. 'This sounds ideal. I'm sure Peter will feel a lot happier if he knows exactly where he's going.'

'Precisely.' Tom followed her across the room, bending so that he could point out a paragraph that was particularly relevant. 'They will even introduce him to the members of staff who'll be looking after him. That's probably more important than anything else. If Peter knows the nurses and doctors, etcetera, he'll be less likely to worry.'

'I'm sure you're right,' Hannah agreed tersely, anxious to put a little distance between them. She went to step back then realised that Tom had beaten her to it and already moved away. He smiled at her but she couldn't fail to see the wariness in his eyes.

'If I were you, I'd give them a call right away, Hannah. The sooner you get it organised the better.'

'Of course,' she murmured, wondering why he appeared so on edge. He'd probably realised that he'd been crowding her, she decided, impinging on her personal space. However, logical though it sounded, she wasn't convinced it was the answer and it bothered her. 'I'll do it now, so long as you don't think Simon will mind.'

'Of course he won't mind. He's gone out on a call but, believe me, he would never have taken you on if he didn't have faith in your judgement.'

'That's good to know.'

Hannah headed for the door, relieved to make her escape. Being around Tom seemed to confuse her for some reason and she didn't appreciate feeling this way. She liked order in her life, not uncertainty, although she was trying not to be as rigid in her outlook as she'd used to be. As she had discovered when she'd been expecting Charlie, not everything went according to plan.

The thought still had the power to hurt. She couldn't help feeling guilty about the way she had tried so hard to structure every aspect of her life. If *she'd* been more flexible then Andrew might not have been so uncompromising too, she thought for the umpteenth time, then sighed when she realised how unlikely that was.

'So how do you feel about us holding the fort while Simon and Ros visit their daughter?'

'I suppose it would make sense,' Hannah said, pausing reluctantly.

'But?' He gave a short laugh. 'There was a definite "but" in there if I'm not mistaken.'

'Was there?' He was far too astute, she realised with a sinking heart. She summoned a smile, keen to convince him that she wasn't the least bit worried by the thought of them working together. 'I suppose I'm a little concerned at the thought of being so new to the practice. It takes a while to find your feet and I wouldn't like to make any major blunders.'

'I'm sure you're far too professional to commit any blunders.'

He returned her smile but once again she could see the wariness in his eyes. It struck her all of a sudden that if she had a problem with Tom then he had a problem with her too. The thought was unsettling because she didn't want there to be *any* issues between them, nothing to make either of them more aware of the other, and she hurried on. 'Let's hope so. Anyway, what about you? Would you be able to delay taking up your new job?'

'Yes, I expect so.' He shrugged. 'Benedict—he's the director of the clinic I'm going to work at—is a friend from way back. I'm sure he would agree to let me start a few weeks later if I explained the situation to him.'

'In that case, there doesn't appear to be a problem.' She gave a light laugh, determined to nip things in the bud. Maybe she *did* find him attractive but so what? She was a grown woman, a mother as well, and she wasn't going to allow herself to get carried away! 'If Ros and Simon do decide to go, I'm sure we'll cope.'

'I'm sure we will too,' Tom murmured. He glanced round when the phone rang, hating the fact that he felt so relieved to be interrupted. He knew it was ridiculous to be so aware of her, but he couldn't seem to stop. Even learning that she was a mother—a definite no-no in his book—

hadn't dampened his interest. As soon as he was near her, common sense flew right out of the window.

It was a worrying thought and Tom knew that he needed to take it on board. Normally, he was the one who called the shots, the one who was always in control, but not this time, it seemed. He needed to get himself back on track and there was no time like the present. He smiled coolly at her, hoping that she couldn't tell how on edge he felt. 'I'd better get that.'

'Of course.'

She didn't say anything else before she left the room so there was no basis for thinking that she was as relieved as he was to put an end to the conversation. Tom lifted the receiver to his ear and listened while the caller explained that the dog had eaten his prescription. It was the sort of anecdote he normally relished, but he found it difficult to concentrate that day. Was Hannah as confused by her feelings as he was by his?

'Are you still there, Doctor?'

'I...um...yes.'

Tom dragged his mind back to the missing prescription and told the caller to come into the surgery and collect another one. He printed it out and left it in the tray then headed out to the corridor. He had to stop thinking about Hannah all the time. If it did turn out that they would be working together for longer than expected then he needed to put things into perspective. It shouldn't be difficult. He just had to remember that he was incapable of being faithful to *any* woman. He was genetically programmed to play the field like generations of his family had done before him. So long as he remembered that, everything would be fine, but if he ever imagined that he could break the cycle...

He cut off that thought. He couldn't change who he was, couldn't erase his heritage, the bad bits or the good. He had tried to do so once before and had failed miserably, and he certainly wasn't going to try it again. No matter how tempted he was, he wouldn't get involved with Hannah, especially when there was a child on the scene.

Children needed stability more than anything

else. They needed people who would stay around while they were growing up and he couldn't promise to do that. Oh, he might *think* he could but, if push came to shove, would he? Could he? Or would the family genes rise to the fore and he'd turn out exactly like the rest of them—incapable of making a commitment and sticking to it?

Tom squared his shoulders. It was a risk he wasn't prepared to take. No matter how attracted he was to Hannah, she was off limits.

# CHAPTER THREE

IT WAS just gone six when Hannah arrived at the nursery to collect Charlie. Simon had insisted that she and Tom should split her evening list, which meant she had managed to get away earlier than expected. Now, as she rang the bell, she found herself wondering why she had been so reluctant to let Tom help her. After all, the world hadn't come to an end because he had seen some patients for her!

'Oh, hi, Hannah. Come on in. Charlie's in the playroom—we can't get him out of the sand tray. He loves it!'

Lucy Burrows, one of the nursery nurses, laughed as she opened the door. Hannah briskly dismissed the thought that she had overreacted as she followed Lucy inside. The sooner she accepted that Tom was just someone she worked with the better. Now, as she paused in the doorway and watched Charlie giggling happily, she was overwhelmed with relief.

Taking Charlie away from everything he knew had been a gamble. Children thrived on stability and she'd been afraid that the move would unsettle him, but so far everything seemed to be working out surprisingly well. He seemed to have settled into the tiny cottage she had rented down by the harbour and he seemed equally happy here at the nursery. After what they had been through in the past year, it was hard to believe that their lives might be changing for the better. If only Andrew had stuck around, surely he would have realised that having a child with talipes wasn't the disaster he imagined?

Hannah's mouth compressed as she went over to her son. The likelihood of her ex altering his views was zero. From the moment they had discovered during her pregnancy that there was a problem with Charlie's feet, Andrew hadn't wanted anything to do with him. He had wanted a perfect child and he had made that clear.

'Hello, darling. Are you having a lovely time?' Hannah crouched down beside the little boy. With his dark brown curls and deep blue eyes, Charlie looked a lot like Andrew. It had hurt at first to see the resemblance, but she had learned to harden her heart. It took more than shared genes to be a *real* father.

Charlie gurgled in delight when he saw her. Hannah picked him up, inhaling his lovely warm baby smell. Even though she needed to work to support them, she missed him so much whenever they were apart.

'He's been as good as gold,' Lucy told her. 'You'd think he'd been coming here for ages, not that it was his first day.'

'That's a good boy.'

Hannah gave Charlie a kiss as she hitched him more securely onto her hip. Although the casts on his legs were lightweight ones, they were still cumbersome and made carrying him rather awkward. She collected his bag and took him out to the car. Digging into her pocket, she tried to ease out the keys but, with Charlie straddling her hip, it wasn't easy. She groaned when she ended up dropping them on the ground.

'Here, let me get them for you.'

All of a sudden Tom was there and she jumped. He smiled as he picked up the bunch of keys. 'I'll get the door for you as well.'

He unlocked the car and opened the rear door, standing back while she strapped Charlie into his seat. She straightened up, forcing herself to smile when he dropped the keys into her hand. Maybe it was the shock of seeing him when she'd least expected it, but her heart was racing again.

'Thanks. You could do with an extra pair of hands when you have a baby,' she said, lightly.

'So I can see.' He smiled back, his deep blue eyes crinkling attractively at the corners. With his tanned skin and athletic build, not to mention that air of confidence he exuded, he must have women fighting to go out with him, she thought, then wondered why the idea made her feel so dejected.

'Well, I'd better get off,' she said, opening the driver's door before any more foolish thoughts could infiltrate her mind. She didn't *want* to go out with him—it was the last thing she wanted! 'Charlie will want his tea.'

'Of course.' He glanced at his watch and grimaced. 'I'd better get my skates on too. I was supposed to be at the lifeboat station for six and it's five past already.'

Hannah paused. 'Are you part of the lifeboat crew?'

'No. I'd love to be, but the fact that I spend most of my time working abroad means it isn't possible.' He shrugged. 'I'm filling in for Simon tonight. He teaches first aid to the crew. There's a couple of new guys who've just started and they need to complete the course as part of their training.'

'Oh, I see.' Hannah hesitated but there was no way she could avoid offering him a lift when she was heading that way. 'I'm going that way so why don't you hop in? It'll save you some time.'

'Oh, I wouldn't want to take you out of your way...'

'You aren't.' She summoned a smile when she

realised how sharp she'd sounded. However, his reluctance to get into the car had stung. 'I'm renting a cottage down by the harbour so I'm going that way.'

'Oh! Right. Then thank you.'

He strode around the car and slid into the passenger seat. Hannah started the engine and pulled out into the traffic. Although the roads were nowhere near as busy as they were in London, she was surprised by the number of vehicles there were about.

'It's a lot busier than I expected,' she observed, easing round a car and caravan combination that was partially blocking the road.

'We're coming into the holiday season. By the middle of July, you won't be able to move in the town centre—it'll be one big traffic jam.'

'Really?' She frowned. 'I had no idea that Bride's Bay was so popular with the tourists.'

'All the towns along this stretch of coast are tourist magnets.' Tom smiled at her. 'You'll learn to live with it, as everyone does. Yes, it does get hectic at times, but the plus side is that the holidaymakers bring a lot of money into the town.'

'Which can only be a good thing,' she concluded. 'Without the extra income then people would need to move away to find work.'

'Exactly. As it is, most of the folk in Bride's Bay have lived here all their lives. That's what makes it so special.'

His tone was warm and she glanced curiously at him. 'You obviously love the town.'

'I do. I've been coming here since I was a child and I can honestly say that it's my favourite place to be.'

'So why didn't you opt to become Simon's partner?' She slowed to let an elderly couple cross the road and glanced at him. 'I'm sure he would have been delighted.'

'I like variety, which is why I prefer to take short-term contracts.'

It was a reasonable answer yet Hannah doubted it was the whole truth. If Tom loved the town so much then the logical step would be for him to settle down here. She was about to point that out when a loud bang made her jump.

'What on earth was that!' she exclaimed, drawing the car to a halt.

'A maroon. They let them off from the lifeboat station to alert the crew when there's a boat in trouble.' Tom leant forward and pointed through the windscreen. 'Look! You can see the trail of smoke it's left behind.'

Hannah leant forward to look then felt her breath catch when she realised how close they were. There was just the tiniest space separating them and it shrank even more when Tom suddenly turned and she found herself staring into his eyes. She felt a shiver run through her when she saw his eyes darken, turning from sapphire blue to midnight in the space of a heartbeat. When he bent towards her she didn't move, couldn't have done so when it felt as though she was drowning in their indigo depths…

Charlie started to cry when a second rocket exploded and the spell was broken. Hannah took a quick breath as she turned to reassure him, but her heart was racing out of control. If they hadn't been interrupted would she have let Tom kiss her? Because that was where they'd been heading.

Her heart sank as she realised that she would have done. She would have let Tom kiss her, kissed him back, and there was no point denying it. On the contrary, she needed to face the truth, admit that she was deeply attracted to him, and do something about it.

She couldn't get involved with Tom. It was far too soon after what had happened between her and Andrew. Discovering that the one person she should have been able to rely on had let her down had knocked her for six and it would be a long time before she could trust anyone again. Then there was Charlie. She intended to focus all her time and energy on making sure that everything possible was done for him. The child may have been let down by his father but he wasn't going to be let down by her too.

Hannah took a deep breath. Nothing was going to happen between her and Tom, not now. *Not ever.*

Tom could feel the heat that had been pooling in the pit of his stomach turning to ice. He couldn't believe what had happened. One minute he'd been looking through the windscreen and the next…

He swore under his breath as he reached for the door handle. He had come within a hair's breadth of kissing Hannah. That was bad enough, but the fact that he appeared to have so little self-control where she was concerned was far more worrying. He *knew* that she wasn't right for him but it hadn't stopped him. He would have kissed her and to hell with the consequences because kissing her had seemed more important than anything else. It made him see how dangerous the situation was. Hannah could turn his world upside down, if he let her.

'I'll walk from here. It's not far now and it'll be quicker than waiting for the traffic to clear.' He opened the car door, using that as an excuse not to look at her. He didn't appreciate feeling so vulnerable. He had always been in control before, of himself and his relationships, but it appeared that he was putty in her hands.

The thought of her hands being anywhere near him was too much. Tom shot out of the car, pausing briefly, as politeness dictated, to thank her. Maybe he should have simply cut and run but he needed to take charge of what was happening, be proactive rather than reactive. 'Thanks for the lift, Hannah. I appreciate it.'

'It was nothing.'

Her voice was husky and he felt the hair all over his body stand to attention. Even though he really didn't want to have to look at her, he couldn't resist. The lump of ice rapidly melted again when he saw the stunned expression on her face. In that second he knew that if he *had* kissed her, she wouldn't have stopped him!

Quite frankly, it was the last thing he needed to know. Tom slammed the door and headed off down the hill as though the hounds of hell were snapping at his heels. In a way they were, because it would be his own version of hell if he allowed the situation to gather momentum. He took a deep breath as he weaved his way through the crowd that had gathered to watch the lifeboat being launched. He was attracted to Hannah, more attracted to her than he'd been to any woman. She seemed to push all the right buttons, or maybe that should be all the *wrong* ones because he certainly didn't want to feel this way. He was happy with his lot, enjoyed his life free from complications…

Didn't he?

Tom's mouth thinned. He wasn't going down that route. He had to do what was right and for him that meant living his life unencumbered by a wife and a family. It was the only way he could guarantee that he wouldn't turn out like the rest of the Bradburys.

*He* didn't intend to leave behind a string of broken marriages and tawdry affairs. *He* didn't plan to break any hearts or ruin any lives. So maybe he'd thought he could buck the trend once, be the one member of his family who could make a marriage work, but he'd soon discovered he was mistaken. How long had his engagement lasted? Two months? Three? Definitely no longer. As soon as he'd realised he was losing interest, he had broken it off.

It had been a salutary lesson, however, and one he needed to remember. Attraction could and did wane. Maybe he was attracted to Hannah at this very moment, but in a week or so's time it could be a different story. It wasn't fair to Hannah to start something that was doomed to failure. It wasn't fair to him either! He didn't need this kind of pressure. He didn't need the worry of constantly wondering if he would hurt her. He wanted to get on with his life and enjoy it, and if that meant staying single then so be it.

Hannah gave Charlie his tea then knelt on the rug and played a noisy game of cars with him. Charlie loved it when they crashed into one another, laughing loudly when his red plastic fire-engine sent her little white ambulance skittering across the floor.

'You're going to be a demon driver when you grow up, my boy,' she smilingly admonished him as she retrieved both vehicles.

Charlie gurgled happily as he sent the toy fire-engine spinning across the room closely followed by the ambulance. Although the casts on his legs meant he couldn't crawl, he had developed his own technique for getting about which involved shuffling on his bottom. Hannah chuckled as she watched him make his way towards the toys.

'You're a determined little chap. I'll say that for you.' She went to help him get the ambulance, which had rolled under a chair, then paused when someone knocked on the front door. 'I won't be a second, darling,' she said, veering off to answer it. There was a young man outside wearing bright yellow oilskins and he smiled uncertainly at her.

'Are you Dr Morris?'

'Yes, that's right. What can I do for you?'

'I'm Billy Robinson, one of the lifeboat crew. Tom asked me to fetch you. We've got two casualties at the station and he needs a hand.' He looked past her and grinned when he saw Charlie. 'Tom said you had a little 'un and to bring him along. There's plenty of folk there who'll be more than happy to look after him for you.'

'In that case, of course I'll come,' Hannah agreed immediately. 'I just need to fetch my bag from the kitchen.'

She hurried back through the tiny sitting-room into the equally compact kitchen. Her medical bag was on the table and she quickly checked that she had everything she needed. When she went back, Billy was holding Charlie, who was laughing happily up at him.

'He seems to have taken to you,' Hannah observed as she shut the front door.

'Oh, I'm well used to kids,' Billy told her cheerfully. 'There's seven of us at home and I'm the oldest, so I've done my share of babysitting.'

Hannah laughed at the rueful note in his voice. He seemed a pleasant young man and she didn't have any qualms about letting him carry Charlie the short distance to the lifeboat station. The doors were open and she hurried inside, taking in the scene that met her. Tom was kneeling beside a middle-aged man, setting up a portable defibrillator, whilst two of the lifeboat's crew were performing artificial respiration on him. It was

obvious they had everything under control so she
hurried over to the second casualty, a woman.
There was another crew member with her and
Hannah knelt down beside him.

'I'm Dr…' She paused and corrected herself.
'I'm Hannah Morris. Can you give me some idea
what's happened to her?'

'Nice to meet you, Hannah. I'm Jim Cairns and
this here is Marilyn Baines. She and her husband
were out on their yacht when the rudder broke
and they ran aground on some rocks. From what
I can gather, the main mast broke and hit her on
the head.'

'Right.' Hannah bent over the woman. 'My
name's Hannah and I'm a doctor. I need to ex-
amine you, Marilyn, if that's all right?'

'Ye…' Marilyn tried to speak but it was obvious that she was still very woozy from the blow
to her head.

'Just relax.' Hannah smiled reassuringly as she
set about examining her, starting with the injury
to her head. It was obviously tender because Marilyn winced when she gently probed it. 'Sorry.

It's a nasty blow and you'll need a CT scan at the hospital.'

'Clive…how is he?' the woman managed to ask.

Hannah gently eased her back down when she tried to sit up. 'Dr Bradbury is with him. Let's concentrate on you for now.'

She carried on, noting down a broken left wrist and dislocated left shoulder. There could be damage to the left humerus as well but that would need to be confirmed when an X-ray was done. There was no doubt that the poor woman was in a great deal of pain so Hannah drew up 10 mg of morphine.

'I'm going to give you something for the pain, Marilyn. Have you had morphine before?'

'No,' Marilyn whispered.

'Sometimes it can make you feel a bit queasy but it's nothing to worry about.' She swabbed the woman's good arm and slid in the needle. The drug took effect almost immediately, although she waited a couple of minutes to see how Marilyn had tolerated it before she set about strapping her wrist and stabilising her shoulder ready for transfer to the hospital.

'How long before the ambulance gets here?' she asked, glancing at Jim.

'The helicopter is on its way,' a familiar voice answered from behind her.

Hannah took a deep breath before she turned, determined that she wasn't going to allow Tom to upset her equilibrium again. He's just a colleague, she reminded herself. Just someone you work with. However, as her gaze skimmed up the long legs and narrow hips before coming to rest on a firmly muscled chest, she realised with a sinking heart that Tom could never be *just* anyone.

She had tried to tell herself that it was purely physical attraction she felt, but it wasn't true. Tom appealed to her on many different levels, ranging from his innate warmth to the consideration he showed to other people. She only had to remember how concerned he'd been about Peter Granger to know that it wasn't an act either. He genuinely wanted to do his best for people, wanted to help them, and that was very appealing.

It was also in marked contrast to Andrew's attitude. Her ex had always put himself and his needs first, as she knew to her cost. However, she sensed that Tom didn't do that, that, despite his playboy lifestyle, he cared about other people. It all added up to one seriously attractive package and the thought scared her.

She might not like the idea, certainly hadn't wished for it to happen, but she had a feeling that Tom was about to take on a far more important role in her life than that of colleague.

# CHAPTER FOUR

'IT WILL be faster if the transfer is made by helicopter.' Tom fixed a smile to his mouth. He had made his decision to keep Hannah at arm's length and he intended to stick to it. He blanked out the thought that the length of his arm wasn't *that* far and carried on. 'It'll cut almost half an hour off the journey time.'

'I see.'

Hannah stood up, making it clear that she wanted to speak to him in private, and he reluctantly followed her. He made a rapid calculation, stopping when he judged himself to be just beyond touching range. There was no point taking *any* chances.

'How bad is he?' she asked, glancing over to where one of the crew was keeping watch over his patient.

'Not good. He's had an infarc—a bad one too—and he needs to be in the coronary care unit ASAP. Although we managed to get his heart started again, there's definite signs of arrhythmia.'

'As you say, he needs urgent treatment.'

'He does. How about your patient?' Tom kept his tone light but even then he feared it wasn't anywhere near as bland as Hannah's as she outlined the woman's injuries. Was she merely better at hiding her feelings or was the explanation far more simple? Had he made a mistake about her being interested in him?

The thought should have reassured him. It didn't. In fact, it felt like a kick in the guts to wonder if he had misinterpreted her response to that near-miss kiss. He'd thought that she had welcomed his advances, whereas she had probably been so shocked that she hadn't resisted! The thought made him wince and he saw her look at him in concern.

'Are you all right?'

'Fine. Just my stomach rumbling.' He gave her

a tight smile, cursing his own stupidity. He should be rejoicing because he'd been let off the hook, not feeling down in the dumps because she wasn't interested! 'I skipped lunch and haven't made it as far as supper.'

'Me too. Well, I did sneak a piece of toast off Charlie's plate so I've fared a little better than you.'

She smiled back and this time Tom could see a hint of something in her eyes. What it was he had no idea and didn't investigate. However, his spirits rose a fraction and he grinned at her.

'We're a right pair, aren't we?'

'I…um… If you say so.'

Thankfully, the roar of an engine announced the arrival of the helicopter so he was spared having to reply. He went back to his patient and got him ready for the transfer. Hannah was doing the same, getting her patient ready to be transferred to hospital. She worked quickly and methodically, sorting everything out with the minimum of fuss. As well as being both beautiful and sexy, she was a damn fine doctor, Tom thought, and sighed.

What a beguiling combination. No wonder he was having such a hard time keeping his distance.

Hannah handed over her patient, briefly reporting her findings to the crew: head injury, which would need a CT scan doing; fractured left wrist; forward dislocation to the left shoulder; and possible fracture to the left humerus. Then it was Tom's turn.

She stepped aside as he succinctly explained what had happened to Clives Baines and what treatment the man had received. His voice was as confident as ever. When it came to medical matters, he obviously knew his stuff; however, when it came to anything else, she could only speculate.

What was he like as a lover? she wondered. Would he be tender, caring and patient? Or would he be eager, greedy and determined to satisfy his own needs? Maybe he would be a mixture of both—tender and giving but also eager and demanding as he drew a response from his partner.

Hannah shivered. She didn't want to think about such things but now that she'd started it was difficult to stop. A picture of Tom, lying naked in bed, sprang into her mind, but the picture wasn't complete. There was no one lying beside him and she didn't dare fill in the gap when she knew whose face she would see. That would be a step too far, picturing herself lying beside him.

'Right. That's all sorted. Do you want to take Charlie outside so he can watch the helicopter taking off?'

All of a sudden Tom was standing beside her and she hurriedly applied a mental eraser to the images in her head. 'Good idea. I'm sure he'll love it.'

She felt quite proud of herself when she heard how calm she sounded. If she could maintain this kind of balance then everything would be fine, she assured herself as she went to collect her son, who was playing a noisy game of pat-a-cake with Billy. Maybe she was attracted to Tom but so long as she recognised the fact, she could deal with it.

'Thanks for looking after him,' she said, scooping a reluctant Charlie into her arms. 'I hope he's not been too much trouble.'

'He's been as good as gold,' Billy assured her.

'Pity about those casts on his legs. They must be a real nuisance for him.'

'They'll be coming off soon,' Hannah explained, and Billy's face brightened.

'That's good to hear. He'll have to come round to our house then and play with my little brother. He's just turned one so they're much of an age.'

Billy said goodbye and left. Hannah frowned when she heard him asking one of the other men if he fancied a pint.

'Something wrong?'

She glanced round when Tom joined her. 'Not really. I was just a bit surprised when Billy mentioned he had a little brother a few months older than Charlie.'

'His mum was more than a bit surprised when she found out she was pregnant again!' Tom laughed. 'There's a ten-year gap between the baby and the next child so it came as a bolt out of the blue.'

'It must have done,' Hannah replied, smiling as she followed him outside. The helicopter had landed in a nearby field and they were just in time to watch it taking off.

'Look,' Tom said, lifting Charlie out of her arms so he could see over the top of the crowd. 'Helicopter. Whee!'

Hannah wasn't sure how to react. Tom hadn't asked her permission to hold Charlie yet it seemed churlish to complain when it was obvious that her son was enjoying himself. She stood silently beside them, thinking how wonderful it would have been if it had been Andrew holding him, Andrew playing the doting father; Andrew accepting him for what he was, not what he'd wanted him to be.

'That was fun, wasn't it, tiger?' Tom swung Charlie round to face him, laughing when the little boy grabbed his nose. 'Hey, that's quite a grip you've got, young man. Can I have my nose back, please?'

He gently released the baby's fingers then balanced him on his hip as he forged a way through the crowd. Hannah shrugged off the moment of introspection as she hurried after them.

'I'll take him now, thanks. He's rather heavy.'

'All the more reason for me to carry him when you've got your bag to lug home.' Tom paused and glanced at her empty hands. 'You are taking it home, I suppose?'

'Oh, er, yes, of course.' Hannah felt herself blush when she realised that she hadn't given a thought to her medical bag. Bearing in mind that it contained a variety of drugs and expensive equipment, she should have been more careful.

'We'll wait here while you fetch it,' Tom told her. 'I'll show Charlie the fishing boats. He'll love them.'

He went over to the harbour wall, leaving her hovering in a sort of no-man's land. She wanted to go after him and insist he give back her son, while on the other hand she needed to fetch her bag. In the end duty won and she hurried back inside the lifeboat station. Jim Cairns was standing guard over her case and he smiled at her.

'Here it is, Hannah. No one's touched anything.'

'Thanks, Jim. I'd forget my head if it wasn't screwed on tight.'

It was obviously the right thing to say because

he laughed. Hannah had a feeling that her lapse had created a bond between them and it was something she would take on board. It didn't always need perfection to make a situation turn out right.

Tom placed Charlie on his knee as he sat down on the harbour wall. The baby seemed entranced by the scene, waving his chubby little fists as he watched the boats set off for an evening's fishing, and Tom smiled. He'd had very little to do with any children outside his work and it was fascinating to observe Charlie's reaction. Even at such a tender age, Charlie was taking everything in, his head turning this way and that as he watched the boats leave the harbour. It was growing dusk and when some of the boats turned on their lights, Charlie gave a little squeal of excitement.

Tom laughed. 'You like this, don't you, tiger?' He buzzed the top of the baby's head with a kiss, surprised by the sudden rush of longing that assailed him. He had long since ruled out the possibility having children yet all of a sudden he found himself thinking how wonderful it would be to watch his child discovering the world. There must be a special kind of magic seeing everything through a child's eyes and he couldn't help wishing that he could experience it for himself. Maybe he shouldn't rule out the possibility of him having a family at some point?

The thought was contrary to everything he had always believed. Tom pushed it aside when Hannah came to join them. He patted the wall, doing his best to behave as though nothing had happened even though it had. Could he really see himself as a father? It was the ultimate commitment, after all, and normally he would have shied away from the idea. However, he couldn't deny that for the first time ever it held a definite appeal.

'Sit yourself down while we finish watching the boats.' He summoned a smile, determined that he wasn't going to get carried away. Maybe the idea did appeal at the moment but he could very easily change his mind.

The thought should have set him back on course faster than anything else could have done but Tom found it lingering at the back of his mind as they watched the last few boats set sail. Charlie gave a little sigh, obviously worn out by all the excitement, and Tom took it as his cue that they should leave. Standing up, he swung the baby into his arms, somewhat surprised by how natural it felt to carry him.

'Shall I take him now?' Hannah suggested, but he shook his head.

'No, we're fine, aren't we, tiger?' He dropped another kiss on the baby's head and heard her sigh softly.

'Thank you.'

'What for?' he asked in surprise.

'For looking after him.' She paused then hurried on. 'For accepting him for who he is.'

Tom frowned, unsure what she meant. 'Who he is?'

'Yes. Some people see the casts and can't see past them.' She shrugged. 'They treat him differently.'

'More fool them.' He settled the little boy more comfortably in his arms, surprised by how protective he felt. 'Anyone would be proud to have a lovely little fellow like this.'

'Anyone except his father.'

Tom could hear the pain in her voice and for the first time in his life he had no idea what to say. He, Tom Bradbury, master of the glib response, the bon mot, the pithy retort, was struck dumb. Charlie's father wasn't proud to have a beautiful little boy like this?

'It's time I went home. Charlie's usually in bed by now.'

Hannah swept the child out of his arms and started up the hill, her head held high, her back rigid, and Tom's heart began to ache. Although he had no idea what had happened between her and the baby's father, it didn't take a genius to work out that whatever it was still hurt her. The thought unlocked his tongue and he hurried after her.

'At least let me carry your bag.' He whipped it out of her hand, not giving her time to object, as he knew she would. Hannah was hurting and hurting badly and whilst he didn't mind being the whipping boy for her anger, he refused to stand aside and watch her struggle.

They walked back from the harbour in silence. Tom guessed that she was not only upset about what Charlie's father had done but about the way she had reacted. She was a very private person and the last thing she must want was to have to explain the situation to him.

For some reason the thought made him even more determined to draw her out and that surprised him. Normally, he didn't involve himself in other people's affairs. However, discovering what had happened to Hannah and—possibly— doing something to help her seemed far more important than maintaining his neutrality. He cared that she was upset. He cared that she'd been hurt. And it was a strange experience to feel this way.

They reached her house and stopped. Hitching Charlie more securely onto her hip she went to bend down but Tom stopped her.

'I take it the key is hidden under that plant pot?' He didn't wait for her to reply as he picked up the key. He shook his head as he slid it into the lock.

'That would be the first place any burglar worth his salt would look.'

'I'll find somewhere else if it bothers you so much,' she retorted.

Tom didn't take offence. If she needed to vent some of her anger, his shoulders were broad enough to take it. Pushing open the door, he stepped aside with a bow. 'After you, madam.'

Hannah stopped dead, her green eyes glittering as she stared back at him. 'I can manage from here, thank you. You don't need to come in.'

She held out her hand for her bag only just then Charlie started to wriggle and almost slipped from her grasp. Tom raised a brow and saw her flush. Swinging round, she stomped inside, leaving him to follow if he chose, which he did. Dropping her case onto a chair, he looked around. Honey-coloured walls and an eclectic mix of furniture gave the room a wonderfully cosy feel. He found himself suddenly filled with envy. It must be marvellous to have a home like this, a place you would look forward to coming back to.

'I like what you've done to the place,' he said

simply, because it would be wrong to tell her that. It hinted at a loneliness he refused to admit to. 'I've been in this cottage before, when the previous tenant fell down the stairs, and it certainly didn't look like this then.'

'I had a local firm in to decorate before I moved in. It needed updating.'

'It certainly did.'

Tom laughed as he took another look around the room. There were windows at both ends and he could imagine how the sunlight would reflect off those honey-coloured walls during the day. It struck him all of a sudden that not one of the expensive apartments he'd lived in over the past few years could hold a candle to this tiny cottage. It took love and commitment to turn a place into a home, and Hannah was blessed with both.

'I'm sorry but I need to get Charlie settled for the night.'

Her voice held just enough of an edge to remind him that he was persona non grata, and Tom swiftly returned his thoughts to what really mattered—Hannah herself. Maybe she didn't want him there but something told him that she needed to talk.

'Fine. You go ahead.' He sat down on the sofa and smiled innocently up at her. 'If there's anything I can do, give me a shout.'

She hesitated, obviously torn between ordering him to leave and behaving with at least a modicum of good manners. In the end manners won. Swinging round, she marched up the stairs, the sound of her footsteps making her true feelings abundantly clear, and Tom grimaced. He didn't usually force himself on people so maybe he should leave?

He stood up abruptly, refusing to allow himself an escape clause. Hannah needed to talk and in the absence of anyone else, he would have to do. He made his way into the kitchen, pausing once again to admire the room. Gleaming white walls, pale blue painted cupboards and an array of colourful china had lifted the place out of its former doldrums. It all looked very inviting and he wasn't someone who was slow to accept an invitation.

Opening the fridge, he rooted through the contents: an onion, some tomatoes, a head of garlic and—wonder of wonders!—a lump of Parmesan cheese. Without pausing to wonder if Hannah would object, he set about making her some supper, frying the onions and garlic in olive oil before chopping the tomatoes and adding them to the pan. He turned down the heat and opened the cupboards, thanking his stars when he discovered a packet of linguini as well as some dried oregano.

'What are you doing?'

The question brought him spinning round and his heart sank when he saw Hannah in the doorway. She had her hands on her hips and her lips pressed tightly together and if that wasn't enough to warn him she was none too pleased, her expression certainly would have done. Tom opted for the conciliatory approach—the gentle smile and soothing voice. Maybe he had overstepped the mark but he didn't want her to throw him out. Not yet. Not until they'd talked and he, hopefully, had found something to say that would help her.

'I thought I'd make you some supper.' He directed her gaze to the pan, wondering why it was so important that she bare her soul to him. Normally, he'd have run a mile to avoid this very situation but this was different.

This was Hannah and she needed him despite what she believed. Growing up in such a dysfunctional family as his, he knew how it felt to have no one to talk to. His parents had been far too busy with their own lives to bother with him so he had learned to keep his counsel. It wasn't that they were deliberately cruel, just self-centred, but he knew how it felt to bottle things up and he didn't want Hannah to do that if he could help her. From what little he'd gleaned so far, she'd been through enough. The thought spurred him on.

'It seems the least I can do bearing in mind that it's my fault you've had nothing to eat tonight.'

'Oh!'

She walked over to the stove and he saw her swallow as she inhaled the rich aroma of tomato sauce. Was her mouth watering? He hoped so. Maybe she wouldn't open up about Charlie's father. After all, he couldn't make her tell him if it wasn't what she wanted, but at least he would have the satisfaction of knowing that she'd had a decent meal.

'It's very kind of you,' she began, but he cut her off.

'It's no big deal. Honestly.' He went over to the stove and stirred the sauce, trying not to let her see that it was a big deal, for him at least. He'd never felt this way before, never felt this need to protect someone. Was it the emotional fragility he sensed in her that made him want to take care of her? He wasn't sure. All he knew was that he wanted to look after her and if the only way he could do that was by feeding her then so be it.

'This'll be ready soon,' he said neutrally, glancing up. 'Is Charlie all settled for the night?'

'Nearly.' She stepped back, making it plain that she didn't want to be too close to him. 'He just needs his bedtime bottle.'

'Why don't you get it ready while I keep an eye on the sauce?' he suggested, refusing to feel hurt. On the contrary, he should be glad that one of them was behaving sensibly.

'All right.' She opened the fridge and took out a carton of formula, pouring it into a baby's bottle and zapping it in the microwave for a couple of seconds. She headed for the door then paused and he could almost feel the reluctance oozing out of her. 'Would you like to stay for supper?'

Tom knew he should refuse. It obviously wasn't what she wanted but he wasn't going to let that deter him. 'That would be great. Thank you.' He smiled reassuringly. 'There's no rush. I'll put the pasta on when you've finished feeding Charlie.'

'Right.'

Tom turned his attention to the pan as she left the room, determined that his mind wasn't going to wander. They would have supper and if Hannah wanted to talk about her ex then she could. However, he wouldn't press her, not for anything, not to talk or to kiss him or to let him make love to her...

He groaned. How long had he held out? One

second? Two? He would have to do better than
that if he was to get through the evening without
making a fool of himself!

# CHAPTER FIVE

HANNAH took a deep breath as she closed the bedroom door. She still wasn't convinced this was a good idea but what else could she have done? Inviting Tom to stay for supper had been the right thing to do, the *natural* thing, in fact. However, she couldn't deny that her nerves were jangling at the thought of them spending any more time together. She was far too aware of him as it was and it certainly wouldn't help to sit across the table from him while they shared the supper he had cooked. It hinted at an intimacy she wasn't ready for... Correction: an intimacy that was never going to happen!

Tom was humming to himself when she went back to the kitchen. He hadn't heard her coming in and it gave her a few seconds to take stock. He'd obviously been busy while she was upstairs, she realised, taking note of the neatly laid table. He'd even found the Parmesan in the fridge and filled an earthenware bowl with shavings. The nutty scent of the cheese mingled with the rich aroma of the sauce made her realise how hungry she was and her stomach rumbled. He looked up and grinned.

'It sounds as though you need feeding. I just have to cook the pasta and it'll be ready.'

'Lovely.' Hannah summoned a smile. Maybe this wasn't how she had envisaged spending the evening but there was no need to worry. She had shared meals with colleagues in the past and nothing had happened, so why should this be any different? 'Is there anything I can do to help?'

'I don't think so… Oh, maybe put out some glasses of water?'

'Actually, I think I've got a bottle of wine somewhere.' She closed her mind to the insidious little voice that was bent on making mischief as she went to find the wine. So maybe it *was* a bit different, having supper with Tom, but she could handle it. 'Ah, yes, here it is.'

She placed the bottle on the counter and fetched the corkscrew. Peeling off the foil, she set to work but the cork refused to budge.

'Let me try. Some of these corks can be the very devil to shift.'

Tom held out his hand and she sighed as she passed the bottle to him. To her mind, he had done enough by making their supper and she didn't want him taking over.

'Damn!' The irritation in his voice brought her eyes to his face and he grimaced. 'I've only managed to break the wretched cork and push it down inside the bottle.'

'Don't worry. It's not a major disaster.' Hannah took the bottle over to the sink, feeling happier now that she had something to do. She found a jug then hunted a tea-strainer out of the drawer and decanted the wine through it. 'I've got most of the bits out so it should be drinkable,' she told him.

'Good.' Tom strained the pasta and added the sauce then tipped it into a dish. He brought it over to the table, using a couple of big spoons to serve out two generous portions. 'I hope it's all right. I've not made it for ages so there's no guarantee as to how it's turned out.'

Hannah forked up a mouthful, nodding enthusiastically by way of reply, and he laughed. 'I'll take that as a good sign, shall I?'

'Uh-huh.' She managed to swallow and smiled at him. 'My compliments to the chef. This sauce is delicious.'

'That's a relief.' He scattered Parmesan shavings over his pasta and dug in. They ate in silence for several minutes before Hannah picked up the jug.

'Will you have some wine?'

'Please.' He moved his glass closer so she could fill it, grinning as he scooped out a stray bit of cork with his finger. 'I won't bother with the chewy bits.' Raising it to his lips, he took a sip. 'Hmm. Very nice, despite its inauspicious start. You obviously know your wine, Hannah.'

'Oh, I can't take any credit for it. Andrew's the wine buff, not me.'

Her response was automatic and as soon as the

words were out of her mouth, she regretted them. She bent over her plate, willing him not to ask any questions. She didn't want to talk about Andrew and what had happened; it was still too raw. She had told nobody the real reason for their break-up; neither her family nor her friends knew the truth. However, she knew that she wouldn't be able to lie to Tom and it was too much, too soon; too dangerous to open up to him. She bit her lip. The fact was that she was far too vulnerable around him.

Tom counted to fifty. Slowly. It was an old ploy, one he'd used to great effect many times. Instead of jumping in and thereby running the risk of regretting it, he gave himself a breathing space to take stock. If he said this or that, how would it impact on him? Would he find himself more involved than he wanted to be? It was a way of separating his emotions and normally it worked like a dream but not tonight. Not with Hannah.

He placed his fork on his plate, seeing the way she avoided his eyes. 'What happened between you and Charlie's father?' Maybe he should have tried a less direct approach but there seemed no point beating around the bush. He wanted to know, she needed to tell him, so it was simpler to leap straight in. 'You said something earlier that implied his relationship with Charlie isn't what it should be. What happened, Hannah? What did he do?'

'It's none of your business.' She started to rise but he reached across the table and captured her hand.

'Probably not.' He looked steadily back at her. 'But I'd still like to know.'

'Why?'

The question was as bald as his had been and he flinched. Did he really want to admit that he cared? Of course not, but now that he'd started this he couldn't stop.

'Because you're hurting. Because you're angry and upset. Because you need to talk to someone.' He paused but he'd already burned his bridges. 'Because I'd like to be that someone, if you'll let me, Hannah.'

Her eyes misted with tears. 'Talking won't

change anything. It certainly won't make Andrew change his mind.'

'I disagree. Oh, not about your ex—as I have no idea what he did, I'm not qualified to comment. However, it could help you and that's the most important thing.' He gave her fingers a gentle squeeze then let her go, knowing that he would find it impossible to do so if he held onto her any longer. 'Has it something to do with the fact that Charlie has talipes?'

'How did you guess?' Her tone was bitter, laced with a pain that cut him to the quick. 'Andrew wanted a perfect baby, you see, a child he could show off to his friends. What he didn't want was a son who had a handicap.'

'But talipes can be corrected! Manipulation, casts, even an operation to sever the ligaments and tendons if those don't work. It's treatable.'

'Yes, it is. But that wasn't good enough for Andrew. He didn't want a child who would need to be *repaired*, as he put it. He wanted one who was perfect from the moment he was born.' She bit her lip and he could see the pain in her eyes. 'When we were told at my twenty-week scan that Charlie would be born with the condition, Andrew wanted me to have a termination.'

It was worse than he'd expected, far, far worse. Tom struggled to find something to say but he knew that whatever he came up with would fall far short of what was needed. In the end he settled on something nonjudgmental, even though it stuck in his throat to offer an excuse for the other man's behaviour.

'Was it the shock? I mean, it's a lot for any prospective parent to take in. Everyone hopes for a healthy baby so that even something like this can seem like a major issue.'

'If that had been the case we could have worked through it. In fact, I thought that was what it was at first—Andrew was simply so shocked that he had no idea what he was saying.' She laughed harshly. 'I was wrong. He didn't change his mind no matter how hard I tried to convince him that it was something we could deal with. He wanted me to get rid of the baby because he wasn't perfect. And I refused.'

'So what happened?' he asked slowly, wondering how she had coped. Not only had she needed to deal with her own shock but she'd lost the support of the one person she should have been able to rely on. Anger rose inside him at the thought of how she'd been let down. If he could have ten minutes alone with her ex… He shoved that thought to the back of his mind. 'Was that why you split up?'

'Yes. Oh, it wasn't the reason Andrew gave, not what he told his friends and colleagues. It wouldn't have made him look good, would it? He chose something a little more palatable…that we'd drifted apart. Obviously, he would help to support the baby financially—if it was his.'

'What! He actually implied that Charlie wasn't his son?'

'Oh, yes.' She smiled tightly. 'Andrew's a barrister and he's very keen on facts. He came up with all sorts of information about how talipes often runs in families. As he was keen to point out, there'd been no child in his family born with the condition.'

'But that's crazy! All right, so there's a greater chance of a child being born with the condition if there's a family history of it, but that isn't always the case.'

'You know that and I know that. Andrew knew it too but it was the perfect excuse. Oh, he was very careful. He just dropped the odd hint, here and there.' She laughed. 'I didn't find out what he was up to until I bumped into one of his colleagues and she let it slip. Suffice to say that he won't be making any more claims like that in the future.'

'And was this before or after Charlie was born?'

'Before. Charlie was born a month later. Andrew still hasn't seen him. So far as he's concerned, Charlie doesn't exist.'

The tears she'd been holding in check suddenly spilled over. Tom got up and came around the table. Kneeling down, he drew her into his arms. 'Shh. It's all right, Hannah. Everything is going to be fine, you'll see.'

She buried her face in his shoulder. Tom guessed that she was embarrassed about breaking down but he knew it would help. Nobody should have to shoulder a burden like this on their own—it wasn't right. He ran his hand over her hair, feeling the silky tendrils clinging to his fingers. He could smell the lemon scent of her shampoo, nothing exotic, just a clean, fresh fragrance that stirred his senses in a way he wouldn't have expected, and suppressed a shudder. He didn't want to alarm her. He wanted to comfort her, make her feel a little bit better. If he could.

She raised her head at last and looked wonderingly at him. 'That's the first time I've cried.'

'Is it?' He smoothed his thumbs over her cheeks, using his own skin to soak up her tears. The shudder he'd been holding back tried again to surface but he stamped on it. No pressure. Nothing to make her feel uncomfortable. And definitely nothing that would hint at the way he would really like to comfort her.

A picture of him pressing his lips to her wet face suddenly filled his head. He would kiss away her tears, soothe her pain with his mouth, comfort her with his hands. He knew he could do all that, but it wouldn't be right. She was at her most vulnerable and he refused to take advantage. He wanted to protect her, cherish her, and the fact that he felt this strongly shocked him. He had always avoided emotional involvement. Not even his erstwhile fiancée had touched him on a deeper level if he was honest. And yet just holding Hannah in his arms filled him with a whole range of emotions.

He let her go and stood up, his heart hammering. He felt both elated and terrified. It was good to know that he wasn't emotionally bankrupt after all, yet he was scared witless at the thought of the damage he could cause. The truth was that he didn't trust himself, couldn't put his hand on his heart and swear that he would feel this way in a year's time. Hell, if his first and only attempt at love was anything to go by, he could forget measuring the time in years and resort to months! So how would he feel in a month's time? Still keen to protect her? Still longing to cherish her and make her happy? He had no idea and that was why this had to stop now.

'You needed to get it out of your system so you can move on,' he said flatly, sitting down. He went to fork up another mouthful of linguine but the pasta had gone cold and was stuck together in an unappetising lump. He put down the fork, wondering if it was an omen. His interest could turn as cold and as stolid as this food.

'I know that. And I will…I am.' She got up and ripped off a piece of kitchen roll. She blew her nose then sat down and picked up her glass, taking a sip of the wine before continuing. 'Moving here was the first step. It was a big decision to leave London but it was the right thing to do. Charlie and I need a fresh start and living here will give us that.'

'Bride's Bay is a good place to live,' he agreed, wanting to add his own endorsement to her plans. Maybe he couldn't offer her the kind of support he yearned to but he could provide encouragement. 'It's a great place to raise a child. I have many happy memories of the times I stayed here when I was growing up.'

'Simon said that he's your godfather?'

He heard the curiosity in her voice and breathed a sigh of relief. It would be easier to turn the conversation away from what she had been through, easier for him. 'That's right. He and my father were at Cambridge together.'

'So your families are friends? That must be nice.'

Tom shrugged. 'Simon and my father have remained friends but my mother was never part of the scene. She works abroad a lot of the time and that's not really conducive to forging close friendships.'

'Oh. I see. What does she do?'

He wasn't sure if he wanted to go into the ins and outs of his family history but he could hardly refuse to answer. 'She's an opera singer. Tessa Wylde...you may have heard of her.'

'Of course I've heard of her!' Hannah looked at him in amazement. 'I can't believe that your mother is Tessa Wylde.' She frowned. 'But I thought she was married to a peer, Lord Something or other?'

'That's right. My father is Lord Bradbury.' He

hated this bit, hated the fact that it altered people's view of him to learn that he was part of the so-called aristocracy. However, apart from an understandable surprise, she didn't seem impressed.

'Fancy that. And do you have a title too?' She grinned. 'Should I address you as sir or my lord?'

'No way!' He laughed. 'Oh, there's probably some archaic form of address if you dig deep enough, but it's not something I ever use. I prefer Tom or Dr Bradbury at a push. My half-brother, Joseph, will inherit the title and he's welcome to it.'

'Half-brother? So your father was married before he met your mother?'

She was obviously keen to learn more and Tom knew that he couldn't fudge the issue even though he would have loved to do so. 'Yes. In fact, my mother is his fourth wife.'

'Good heavens!' She clapped her hand over her mouth. 'Sorry. That wasn't very tactful.'

'Don't worry about it.' He summoned a smile. 'Mother's own track record isn't much better. She was married twice before she met my father. And both of them have had umpteen affairs, both before and after the nuptials. As for Joseph, well, it looks as though he's heading the same way. He's in the process of getting divorced, in fact.'

He shrugged, trying to make light of his family's chequered marital history. 'It's a family tradition. We Bradburys get married, divorced and have affairs at a rate of knots. We're genetically programmed to be unfaithful!'

# CHAPTER SIX

HANNAH wasn't sure what to say. Although Tom was smiling, she sensed it was merely a cover. Was he embarrassed by the thought of his family's behaviour?

She frowned. He didn't strike her as the sort of person who would feel ashamed of other people's actions yet there was definitely something troubling him. It was on the tip of her tongue to ask him when she thought better of it. She didn't want to become involved in his affairs. It was too dangerous.

'They say that you can choose your friends but not your family,' she observed lightly.

'And very true it is too.' He gave her a wide smile but she could tell how false it was. She realised all of a sudden that the charm that was so much in evidence was merely a front to hide his true feelings. Tom kept his emotions strictly to himself. He didn't share them.

It was an intriguing thought, one that might have made her dig deeper if she hadn't decided not to get involved. At the present time she had enough to contend with. She needed to concentrate on making a life for herself and Charlie. Getting inside Tom's skin and discovering what made him tick wasn't an option.

'So what about your family, Hannah? Do you have sisters or brothers?'

'One of each. Sarah is a nurse and Dominic's an engineer,' she told him, relieved to get back onto safer ground.

'I see. And how about your parents—are they still alive?' He prompted her to tell him more, mainly, she suspected, so he wouldn't have to tell *her* anything else, but that was fine.

'Yes, they're both fit and well, I'm happy to say. Dad was in the police. He retired last year and spends as much time as possible fishing. Mum's still working—she's a dinner lady at the local high school and she loves her job. She's planning to stay there as long as she can.'

'It's great if you do a job you enjoy.'

'It is.'

'Do they live in London?'

'No, Liverpool.'

'Really?' His brows rose. 'Weren't you tempted to move back there when you decided to leave London?'

'Not really.' She shrugged. 'It's a long time since I lived there so the ties have been well and truly cut. I wanted to move to the coast for Charlie's sake so that's why I applied for this job.'

'And your family can always come and visit you.'

She nodded, not wanting to explain that she rarely saw them these days. Andrew had always found an excuse whenever she had wanted to visit her parents so that trips home had become increasingly rare in the last few years. She sighed. She'd often wondered if he'd thought that her parents' neat little semi wasn't grand enough but had managed to dismiss the idea. Now it seemed more likely. For Andrew, a visit to her family's modest home would have fallen far short of his ideas of perfection.

It was another black mark against him, a minor one compared to what he had done to Charlie, granted, but something else she should never have allowed to happen. Once again Hannah was struck with guilt for the way she had behaved. She had been so driven by her own need to create a perfect life that she had allowed Andrew to influence her to such an extent that she'd lost touch with her family. She would have to do something to rectify the situation, she decided, always assuming that her parents would forgive her for the way she had behaved.

The conversation seemed to run out of steam after that. When she suggested making coffee, Tom shook his head. 'Thanks but I'll pass on the coffee, if you don't mind.' He pushed back his chair. 'I've a few things to sort out if I'm to start that job in Paris next week.'

'You're still planning to go?' she queried, getting up.

'It all depends on what Simon and Ros decide to do. If they're set on visiting Becky then I'll have to wait until they get back.'

He picked up his plate and took it over to the sink then went back for the bowl but she took it off him. 'Leave that. I'll clear up later.'

'Sure?'

He didn't insist, making her realise that he was keen to leave. Why wouldn't he be? she thought as she led the way through the sitting room. He'd prepared her supper, listened to her tale of woe and offered his support; he'd done more than enough for one evening and far more than she should have let him. She opened the front door, suddenly as eager as he was to bring the evening to an end.

'Well, thanks again for making supper,' she said brightly.

'It was my pleasure.'

He paused in the doorway, the light from the street casting a shadow over his face so that it was hard to see what he was thinking. Hannah stepped closer and maybe he interpreted her action in a way she'd not intended because he suddenly bent and dropped a kiss on her cheek. He drew back and she shivered when she was deprived of the warmth of his mouth.

'It really was a pleasure, too, Hannah.'

He gave her a last smile then stepped out of the door. Hannah hastily closed it, not trusting herself stand there and watch him leave. She had a feeling that she might do something really stupid, like call him back…

She put her hand to her cheek, pressing her fingertips against the spot where his lips had touched, but the heat had gone now. There was just the memory of it in her mind, an echo of sensation, but even that was enough to make her shiver. It had been a typical social kiss to all intents, the sort of kiss people bestowed on friends and acquaintances every day of the week, yet it seemed to have taken on a far greater significance in her mind. Maybe Tom had kissed her as a friend but she knew that even a simple kiss could lead to something more. The scariest thing was admitting that she wouldn't mind if it did.

\* \* \*

'Thanks for the update… Yes, it is a shame, but you win some and you lose some.'

Tom ended the call. It was just gone eight and he'd been getting ready to see his first patient when Jim Cairns had phoned to tell him that Clive Baines, the man who'd been rescued from the yacht, had died during the night. Although Tom wasn't entirely surprised by the news, he found it dispiriting. *Was* there anything else he could have done to help him?

He shrugged off the thought and buzzed for his first patient. Giving in to self-doubt was non-productive and normally not one of his failings. However, he'd felt unsettled ever since he'd left Hannah's house the previous night. Learning what she had been through had affected him more than he had imagined it would do and he was having the devil of a job getting back on even keel. Maybe he *did* want to help her but he was very aware that it could cause more harm than good if he tried.

'Morning, Tom, and how are you today?'

'Still here so that's one for the plus column,' Tom replied as cheerfully as he could when Mitch Johnson came bustling into the room. At a little over six feet in height and almost as round as he was tall, the landlord of The Ship Inn cut an unmistakable figure in the town. Now he plonked himself down on a chair and grinned at the younger man.

'I know what you mean. It's always a good day when I wake up in the morning.' Mitch laughed loudly, enjoying his own joke, and Tom smiled.

'Too right it is. Anyway, what can I do for you today?'

'Simon told me to pop in so you could review my medication. I happened to mention that I've been having a few funny turns of late when he called in for a drink and he was concerned in case it's these new pills I'm taking.'

'What do you mean by funny turns?' Tom asked, bringing up the patient's file on the computer. Mitch had a history of hypertension—high blood pressure— and had been treated with a range of medication over the years. As high blood pressure increased the chances of him having a stroke or developing heart disease, he had regular check-ups both at the surgery and at the hospital. Tom noted that Mitch been seen at the hospital the previous month and that his medication had been changed then.

'I've been finding that everything looks fuzzy, sort of out of focus, if you know what I mean,' Mitch explained. 'I went and had my eyes tested but according to the optician there's nothing wrong with them. Then last week I started with a blinding headache which lasted a whole day. I've not had anything like it before either.'

'Hmm. It sounds as though the new medication could be to blame.' Tom frowned as he checked the name of the tablets. 'I've not come across these before. Let me have a look and see what it says about them.'

He picked up his copy of *MIMS*, which listed all the medications they prescribed, but the one Mitch was taking wasn't included. 'No, they're not in here. They must be very new.' He picked up the phone. 'I'll have a word with the doctor you saw last time you visited the hospital and ask him what he knows about them.'

He put through the call but the doctor in question was in the clinic. Tom asked to speak to the consultant but she was on maternity leave. He hung up. 'Dr Latimer's in clinic so I'll have to phone back later and speak to him. He must be new because I've not come across him before either.'

'That's right. He told me he'd only been working there for just over a month,' Mitch confirmed. 'Usually I see Dr Fairburn but she's on maternity leave.'

'So I believe. Not to worry. We'll soon get it sorted out. In the meantime, I suggest you go back on your old medication. Do you know why Dr Latimer changed it?'

'Not really.' Mitch shrugged. 'To be honest, I felt fine taking the others. I don't know why he decided to change them because my blood pressure's been stable for months.'

'Hopefully, he'll explain his reasons when I speak to him,' Tom said, although he, too, thought it odd that Dr Latimer had prescribed something different. He printed out a script and handed it to Mitch. 'I'll check your BP while you're here. Can you roll up your sleeve?'

He checked Mitch's BP, frowning when he saw the reading. 'It's on the high side, which would explain the headaches you've been having as well as the blurred vision. We need to keep an eye on it so I want you to pop in next week and let Emily check it again.'

'Hopefully, it will have settled down by then.' Mitch rolled down his sleeve and stood up. 'Thanks, Tom. Oh, I heard about that chap you helped last night. Shame he didn't make it.'

'It is.' Tom managed to smile but he could feel the gloom descending on him again and it was very odd. He had long since accepted that he couldn't save everyone; nobody could. He did his best and that was all he could do so why had he taken this case so much to heart? Was it the fact that he hadn't been able to help Hannah either that made him feel so useless?

He sighed as Mitch bade him a cheery goodbye. Hannah had been constantly on his mind. It wasn't just the fact that he felt so useless but everything else, like that kiss, for instance. Why in heaven's name had he kissed her? It had been a crazy thing to do. He had tried to dismiss it as nothing more than a token but in the depths of the night he had woken more than once recalling how soft and smooth her skin had felt, how warm and tempting when he had pressed his lips against it.

A shudder ran through him and he groaned. He had to stop this, had to stop thinking about her. With a bit of luck he would be leaving at the end of the week and that would be the end of the matter. Once he'd put some distance between them he could forget how she made him feel. She would be out of his life for good and that was the best thing that could happen for him and for her.

Hannah worked straight through till lunch then went to the office where Lizzie, the receptionist, was sorting the morning's post. A pretty woman in her thirties with bright red hair and freckles, Lizzie had worked at the practice since she had left school. Now she looked up and smiled.

'How's it going?'

'Fine. I think!' Hannah laughed as she placed the files she had used in the tray.

'Well, from what I've heard you're a big hit. Joyce Cairns was in earlier and she was saying that her Jim had spoken very highly of you,' Lizzie told her.

'That's good to hear.' Hannah smiled back, feeling her pulse leap when she heard footsteps coming along the corridor. She didn't need to check who they belonged to because she recognised Tom's firm tread.

She sighed as she separated a couple of letters that needed posting and placed them in the box. Tom had been on her mind far too much since last night. Even this morning she had found herself thinking about that kiss and how it had made her feel, and it was the last thing she needed. Her emotions had been through the wringer recently and she needed time to recover.

Then there was the fact that Charlie needed so much care and would continue to need it for the foreseeable future. One of the most hurtful things

Andrew had said was that he wasn't prepared to give up his life for a child and it was something she had taken to heart. If her son's own father wasn't prepared to devote any time to him, why should another man wish to do so? She had seen couples go through similar experiences in the course of her work and knew that having a child who needed extra care put a strain on a relationship. She wasn't prepared to subject herself and Charlie to that kind of pressure so that was another reason why she had ruled out having a relationship. However, as Tom came into the room, she found herself thinking that it was a good job he was leaving otherwise she could have had a real problem on her hands.

'Right, that's the morning over so onto round two. I'm down for the house calls this afternoon, I believe.'

Tom dropped his files into the tray and turned. Hannah saw him start when he spotted her and summoned a smile. The last thing she needed was him realising that she'd been standing there, thinking about him.

'Busy, busy, busy. The life of a GP is all go,' she said lightly.

'It is indeed.'

He returned her smile with one that was as bland as hers had been and yet there was something in his eyes that told her he was as aware of her as she was of him. Heat flowed through her and she turned away, afraid that he would notice her reaction too.

'That's right, you're down for the calls today. There's quite a long list, too.' Lizzie picked up a sheet of paper and handed it to him. 'I've put Susan Allsop at the top. She didn't sound at all well when she phoned. Her hubby's away, so I thought it might be best if you made her your first call.'

'Will do.' Tom skimmed through the list. 'This should keep me busy. See you later, folks. Have fun.'

Hannah breathed a sigh of relief when he left. The less time she spent around him the better. She was just about to check the roster to see what she was scheduled for when Simon came bustling into the room.

'I'm glad I caught you before you went for lunch, Hannah. I've just had a word with Tom and asked him to take you with him.'

'Oh, right. I see.' Hannah couldn't keep the anxiety out of her voice and she saw Simon frown.

'It isn't a problem, is it?'

'Of course not.' She dredged up a smile, hating the fact that she was allowing this awareness of Tom to get in the way of doing her job. 'So long as Tom doesn't mind me tagging along, I'm happy to go with him.'

'Good.' Simon smiled at her. 'It'll be easier for you if you have some idea of where everything is.'

'Of course.' Hannah took a deep breath, determined that she wasn't going to let this new development throw her. She would be spending the afternoon with Tom; so what? She was a grown woman and she could handle a couple of hours in his company without doing something she would regret. She closed her mind to what could happen as she smiled at Simon. There was no point thinking about that kiss when there wasn't going to be a repeat! 'It'll be a big help when I have to do the calls by myself.'

'Exactly.' Simon beamed at her. 'Sat nav is all well and good but nothing beats first-hand knowledge. Tom knows the countryside around here almost as well as I do. He'll be the perfect teacher.'

'I'm sure he will.'

Hannah shivered as she made her way to the door. The thought of Tom teaching her anything made her go hot and cold. She collected her case then made her way to the car park. Tom was waiting for her with the engine running. He looked round when she opened the car door and she could tell at once that he, too, had reservations. Tom was as keen to maintain his distance as she was, it seemed.

The thought should have reassured her but it didn't. The fact that he had as big a problem with her as she had with him merely highlighted the danger of them spending time together. However, short of refusing to accompany him, there was nothing she could do.

Hannah took a deep breath and slid into the passenger seat.

# CHAPTER SEVEN

TOM could feel his heart thumping as he put the car into gear and silently cursed himself. He and Hannah weren't going on a date—they were working! The sooner he got that straight in his head, the better.

'Where to first?'

He jumped when she spoke, feeling his heart increase its tempo until it felt as though it was trying to leap right out of his chest. It took every scrap of willpower he possessed to reply calm. 'Susan Allsop's home at Dentons Cove. It's some distance from here, a good fifteen miles, I'd reckon.'

'I hadn't realised the practice's catchment area was so extensive.'

Tom breathed a sigh of relief when Hannah responded in the same no-nonsense tone. So long as they stuck to practicalities, they would be fine. 'It's a lot bigger than you'd get in a city. Obviously there's a higher concentration of people in a city and that determines how big an area each practice covers.'

'Where's the nearest practice to Bride's Bay?'

'Westcombe.'

'Really? That's a long way away,' she said in surprise, twisting round so she could look at him.

'It is.' Tom kept his eyes on the road. Talking he could handle but if he had to spend too much time looking at her... He cut short that thought. He refused to go down the route of speculating what might happen. One, very *chaste,* kiss didn't make a romance. And it certainly didn't mark the beginning of an affair! 'There was another practice further along the coast but it closed last year when the GP who ran it retired.'

'I'm surprised that nobody wanted to take it over.'

He shrugged. 'So many people had moved away to find work that there weren't enough patients to make it a viable proposition.'

'It must have put extra pressure on Simon,' she suggested, and he nodded.

'It did. Most of the remaining patients transferred to his list. That's why Simon was so keen to find a replacement when Margery announced she was leaving. He knew he wouldn't be able to manage with just locum cover.'

'Lucky for me. The job came up at just the right time.'

She gave a little laugh and Tom couldn't resist any longer. He glanced sideways, feeling his pulse leap when she smiled at him. He'd met women who were far more beautiful than her, he thought wonderingly, met, dated *and* slept with them. However, he could honestly say that not one of them had had this effect on him.

'Mmm.' He cleared his throat, determined that he wasn't going to give in to this attraction he felt. Hannah didn't need him messing up her life. He didn't need his life messed up either. He had to fight his feelings no matter how difficult it was. 'Odd how things work out, isn't it?'

'It is.'

There was a strange note in her voice that piqued his interest but he refused to allow himself even the tiniest leeway. So what if she was thinking that if she hadn't taken this job they would never have met? He knew what he had to do and he would stick to it. He wouldn't be responsible for breaking her heart.

They drove in silence after that. Tom knew that he should have spent the time pointing out the various landmarks along the way. However, he didn't trust himself to engage her in conversation. Even the most innocent comment could turn into something far more engaging and he couldn't take that risk. It was a relief when they reached the road leading down to Dentons Cove.

'Susan's house is down here,' he explained as he turned off the main road. 'She and her husband, Brian, bought a couple of old fishermen's cottages a few years ago and turned them into a guest house. They're both artists and they run courses for people interested in painting.'

'I'm sure the courses must be very popular. The view is fabulous,' she said, taking in the vista of sea and sky that greeted them as they drove down the narrow lane.

'It is. It's a favourite spot of mine. No matter what time of the year you come here, the scenery is spectacular.'

'But not spectacular enough to tempt you to move here permanently?'

'No.'

Tom didn't say anything else as he drew up outside the row of cottages. There was no point explaining why he couldn't put down roots. Although he had told her a little about his dysfunctional family, he wasn't prepared to admit how big an influence their behaviour had had on him. Thrusting open the car door, he got out, wishing not for the first time that he'd been born into a normal family. Then he could have been like everyone else. He could have fallen in love, got married, had kids…

He made himself stop right there. He was who he was and that was the end of the matter. He had been perfectly happy with his life, too, until he'd met Hannah. He glanced at her as she got out of the car and felt his heart ache with a sudden sense of loss that shocked him. Having Hannah in his life had never been an option so why did he feel so bereft?

Hannah closed the car door, using the few seconds it took to calm her nerves. Sitting so close to Tom on the drive to the cove had been even more of an ordeal than she had imagined. She was so aware of him that each time he'd moved her pulse had raced. She couldn't recall reacting like this around anyone before, not even Andrew, and the thought made her feel even more rattled. Somehow she had to slot Tom into his rightful place as a colleague. Once she'd done that, everything would be fine.

'Did Lizzie give you a print-out of Susan Allsop's recent notes?' she asked, adopting her most professional tone.

'She did. Sorry. I should have let you take a look at them.' He handed her the sheet, waiting patiently while she acquainted herself with the patient's medical history. She nodded when she came to the end.

'A history of diabetes, which seems to be under control.'

'Yes. Susan was diagnosed shortly after she moved here and has been very good about monitoring her blood glucose levels. She also sticks to the diet the diabetes team at the hospital recommended and so far has had no real problems.'

'It says here that she had an appointment at the surgery last week to check her blood pressure.'

'That's right. Emily, our practice nurse, saw her. She deals with all the routine checks. Susan comes into the surgery every three months to have her BP checked as diabetics have a higher-than-average risk of developing hypertension, as you know.'

Tom took the print-out off her and Hannah sucked in her breath when their hands brushed. It took her all her time to concentrate as he continued when she could feel her fingers tingling from the contact.

'Everything was fine according to Emily's notes so I'm not sure what's happened since then. We'd better go and find out.'

He slid the sheet into his case and knocked on the cottage door. Hannah stood to one side, distracting herself from any more such nonsense by admiring the colourful window boxes. Tom knocked again, louder this time, looking puzzled when nobody answered his summons.

'That's strange. I'm sure Susan wouldn't have gone out when she'd requested a home visit.'

'Maybe she's at the back of the house and hasn't heard you.'

'Could be.' Tom knocked a third time, but still failed to get a response. He looked concerned when he turned to her. 'I don't like this one little bit. I'll try going round to the back of the house and see if I have more success there.'

'I'll come with you,' Hannah offered immediately, following him as he walked briskly to the end of the row of cottages and turned down a narrow path. It led to the rear gardens, each one neatly fenced off from its neighbour with latticework panels. Tom counted the gates as they passed them.

'This should be it.' He undid the latch and let

himself into the garden. Like the window boxes, it was a riot of colour and she sighed wistfully as she followed him to the back door.

'I wish my garden looked like this. The only thing growing there at the moment is weeds.'

'You can't hope to make everything perfect all at once,' he said lightly. 'You've done wonders with the inside of the house, don't forget.'

'You're right.' Hannah smiled, appreciating the timely reminder not to set her sights too high. She was done with aiming for perfection all the time and would be content that she had achieved so much. 'Thank you for reminding me.'

'My pleasure.' He gave her a crooked grin then turned to the door, rapping loudly with his knuckles on the lavender-painted wood. He seemed completely focussed on the reason for their visit but she had seen the awareness in his eyes and knew that he was having as hard a time as she was keeping his feelings in check. Maybe they did both know it would be a mistake to get involved but knowing a thing didn't always rule out it happening.

Hannah shivered. All it would take was a moment of weakness and they could find themselves in a situation they would both regret.

Tom kept his attention on the door. He knew that he had given himself away and hated to think that he might have made Hannah feel uncomfortable. If only he could press a button and erase his feelings, he thought as he knocked again. Then life could return to normal.

The thought was less appealing than it should have been. However, he really didn't want to dwell on the idea that being fancy-free wasn't all it was cracked up to be. He turned to Hannah, determined that he wasn't going to make a difficult situation worse. 'I'm going to try one the neighbours and check if they've seen Susan today. There's no way that she would have gone out when she knew we were coming.'

'I agree.' Hannah stepped around him and peered through the window. 'There's no sign of her but there's a cup of tea and a plate of sandwiches on the table. It looks as though she never got round to eating her lunch.'

'Not a good sign,' Tom said grimly. He headed down the path and went to the cottage next door. An elderly man answered his knock and Tom smiled at him. 'I'm sorry to bother you but have you seen Mrs Allsop today? I'm Tom Bradbury. I'm a doctor at Bride's Bay Surgery.'

'I know who you are, son. You saw my wife last year, Edith Harris, remember? You sorted out her arthritis for her.'

'Of course I remember Mrs Harris,' Tom confirmed. 'How is she doing?'

'Fine. She says she's not felt so well for years.' The old man frowned as he peered over the fence. 'You're looking for Susan, are you?'

'That's right. I've tried the front door and the back but there's no reply. Do you know if she's gone out?' Tom queried.

'I doubt it. Edith was speaking to her yesterday and Susan told her that she wasn't feeling too well—sort of light-headed and dizzy.' The old man reached back inside the house and produced a key. 'We have a key to her house. It's handy if she's out and the meter needs to be read. Why don't we let ourselves in and check that everything's all right, Doctor?'

'That's a great idea, Mr Harris,' Tom said in relief. He moved aside so the old man could lead the way, quickly introducing him to Hannah in passing.

'Nice to meet you,' Mr Harris said politely as they made their way to Susan's door. He inserted the key into the lock but when he tried to open the door it wouldn't budge. 'Something's stopping it,' he said, glancing at Tom.

'Here, let me see if I can open it.' Tom positioned himself in front of the door and pushed as hard as he could. It opened a couple of inches, just enough for him to see a foot through the gap. He turned urgently to Hannah. 'It looks as though Susan has collapsed. We need to get in there, pronto.'

'Let's see if we can open the door a bit more then maybe I can slide inside.'

Hannah hurried to his side, placing her shoulder next to his. Tom sucked in his breath when he felt her breasts brush his back as she moved closer. 'On three,' he said through gritted teeth because this wasn't the time for thoughts like the ones that were dancing around his head. 'One. Two. Three!'

They both pushed as hard as they could and succeeded in opening the door another couple of inches. Hannah slipped off her jacket and handed it to him.

'I should be able to get through there now.' She inched her way through the gap and a moment later he heard the sound of furniture scraping across the floor.

'Are you OK?' he called, wishing that he hadn't let her go first. What if Susan hadn't collapsed? What if she'd been attacked, struck down by someone out to harm her, someone who even now could be lurking in the house? Fear rose inside him and he put his shoulder to the door once more. 'I'm coming in, Hannah. Stand clear!'

This time the door bounced back on its hinges, catapulting him inside. Hannah looked up from where she was kneeling next to Susan and he saw the amusement in her eyes. 'You certainly know how to make an entrance, Dr Bradbury.'

Tom grinned self-consciously as he went to join her. 'I was worried in case there was someone lurking in the shadows.'

'Lurking?'

'Uh-huh. A burglar or someone of that ilk,' he said, dropping to his knees. He checked Susan's pulse, nodding when he felt it beating away, then curled back her eyelids and checked her response to light. Although she was unconscious, her vital signs were good and that was reassuring. Opening his case, he took out a device for testing blood glucose levels. If, as he suspected, there was too little glucose in her blood it could have caused her to collapse and it needed to be checked straight away.

'Ah, I see.' Hannah took an alcohol wipe out of the bag and cleaned Susan's finger so he could take a sample of her blood. 'Well there don't appear to be any bogeymen in here, although rest assured that you'll be the first person I call if I do come across any.'

She was openly laughing now and Tom was assailed by a rush of pleasure at the thought that it was all his doing. He had a feeling that there'd been far too little laughter in her life of late. He grinned back as he spread the blood on a chemically coated strip and popped it into the machine to obtain a reading. He knew that she would see how he felt, yet suddenly he didn't care. He liked her. A lot. And for the first time in his life perhaps he was going to allow his heart to rule his head.

'Fine by me, so long as you promise to return the favour.' His eyes held hers fast for a moment. 'When I wake up in the middle of the night thinking there's a bogeyman under the bed, I hope you'll be there to chase him away, Hannah.'

# CHAPTER EIGHT

'YOU'VE had a hypoglycaemic attack, Susan. In other words, there was too little glucose in your blood and that's why you passed out.'

Tom's voice was gently reassuring as he helped Susan Allsop onto a chair and Hannah sighed. She could do with some reassurance herself. The whole time that she and Tom had been working together to help Susan—administering an injection of glucagon, checking her BP and heart rate—the same disturbing thought had been humming away inside her head: her relationship with Tom had moved onto a whole new level.

'But I've done everything I usually do, taken my insulin and stuck to my diet,' Susan protested. 'I don't understand why this has happened if I've done everything I'm supposed to do.'

Hannah forced herself to focus on what was

happening. There would be time to think about the rest later, although how it would help was open to question. She was attracted to Tom, he was attracted to her—the situation was pretty clear from what she could see. It was how she intended to handle it that needed sorting out.

She pushed that thought to the back of her mind as Tom explained that sometimes glitches occurred. Whilst in no way playing down the seriousness of what had happened, he was obviously trying not to frighten the woman and Hannah found herself thinking what a good doctor he was. A frightened patient didn't respond nearly as well as one who had confidence in the advice they were being given.

'Have your glucose levels fluctuated recently?' he asked finally.

'Not really,' Susan replied hesitantly.

'But your readings have altered?'

'I suppose so.' Susan bit her lip then hurried on. 'I'm afraid I didn't really take that much notice. I've been so busy with Brian being away, you see. We have guests arriving next week and all the bedrooms need repainting. I haven't had time to think about anything else.'

'Which could explain why this has happened,' Hannah put in gently. She smiled when Susan glanced uncertainly at her. 'The extra work you've been doing has affected the balance between the amount of insulin you need and the food you eat. You'd suffer the same effect if you skipped a meal or didn't eat enough carbohydrates.'

'Really?' Susan looked surprised. 'I had no idea. I mean, I know that I have to eat at set times and that I need to be careful about how much carbohydrate I have but I didn't realise that being extra busy could cause a problem.'

'I'm afraid it does have an effect,' Tom agreed. 'That's why it's so important to take note of any changes in your glucose levels. It's the indicator that things aren't as they should be.'

He gave Susan a moment to absorb that then stood up. Hannah stepped aside to let him pass, refusing to let herself dwell on the thought of how good he smelled. She had enough to contend with without that as well. She went and stood by the open door, not sure she could trust herself where he was concerned. Everything about him seemed to be a turn-on, from the way he smiled to the fact that his skin smelled so clean and fresh.

What was it about him that made her aware of things she would never have noticed normally? she wondered as she watched him pack everything back into his case. She had no idea but there was no use pretending that she was indifferent to him when every cell in her body was repudiating the idea. The fact was that Tom affected her more than any man had ever done.

It was a sobering thought. Hannah let it settle in her mind while he explained to Susan that he would make an appointment for her to see the diabetic care team. Even though the current crisis had been dealt with, he felt it would be best if she was given a thorough check-up at the hospital. Susan obviously wasn't happy about the idea but she saw the sense in what he was saying and agreed. He made a quick call to the hospital and fixed up an appointment for her to be seen the following day. Mr Harris had gone to fetch his wife and they insisted that Susan should go back to their house and spend the afternoon with them. Tom had a word with the elderly couple, asking them to phone the surgery if they were at all worried. Although he didn't anticipate any problems, he wanted to be sure that every eventuality was covered. Once they had assured him that they would phone immediately if Susan didn't seem herself, they left.

Hannah followed him back to the car, steeling herself to get through the rest of the afternoon without making a fool of herself. Maybe they were attracted to one another but they were working and that had to take precedence over everything else.

'Where to next?' she asked, determined to set the tone for the rest of the day.

'I'm not sure. Let me take a look at that list and work out which is the best route to take from here.'

He reached over the back of the seat and snared the print-out, frowning as he glanced down the list. Hannah looked away when she felt her stomach muscles quiver. The situation must be serious if she found even a frown arousing!

'The rest of the calls are all in or around Bride's Bay.' Tom glanced up and she hurriedly smoothed her face into a suitably noncommittal expression. Thankfully, he seemed oblivious to what had been going through her mind as he continued. 'We'll head back, do a couple calls on the way, and maybe stop for lunch before we do the rest, if that suits you?'

'I'm happy to work straight through,' she said quickly, not sure if it was wise to risk having lunch together. 'In fact, I'd prefer to get the calls out of the way. There's a few things I need to sort out before evening surgery and it would be a help if we got back early.'

'Fine by me,' Tom agreed.

He started the engine and turned the car around, pointing out the various landmarks along the way, and Hannah breathed a sigh of relief. If they could continue behaving like this then there was no reason to worry. Tom would be leaving at the end of the week so all she had to do was get through the next few days and that would be it. He would be out of her life for good, which was what she wanted...

Wasn't it?

Tom was relieved when the day came to an end. Although he enjoyed working at the surgery because it was such a change of pace from his usual hectic schedule, today had turned into something of an ordeal. He bade Lizzie a brisk goodnight and just as briskly headed out to his car. Maybe it was cowardly but he wanted to avoid running into Hannah if he could.

He sighed as he drove out of the car park. He had never, ever taken evasive action like this before. The women he dated came and went without creating the tiniest ripple in his life. Not even his ex-fiancée had made much impression on him, if he was truthful. But Hannah was different. He would remember her for the rest of his life.

It was a sobering thought. He deliberately expunged it from his mind as he headed into the town centre. Although he usually ate with Simon and Ros, he felt the need to be on his own tonight so he would have supper at The Ship then take in a movie at the cinema. A nice, gory action film would fill in a couple of hours and stop him brooding.

He was almost in the town centre when he saw Hannah's car drawn up by the side of the road. The bonnet was up and clouds of steam were issuing from it. He hesitated a moment, debating the wisdom of playing the good Samaritan, but no matter how much sense it made to drive past, there was no way that his conscience would allow him to leave her stranded.

He drew up behind her car and got out. Walking round to the front of the vehicle, he found Hannah peering under the bonnet. 'Looks like your radiator has blown.'

'So the man from the roadside rescue service informed me,' she said tartly, glaring at him.

Tom held up his hands. 'Hey, don't shoot the messenger.'

'Sorry.' She dredged up a smile but he could tell that she was feeling very stressed.

'Don't worry about it.' He glanced into the car but there was no sign of Charlie. 'You've obviously not made it to the nursery yet. Have you phoned them?'

'Yes. I explained that I'd be late but the problem is that I have no idea how long it will take for the breakdown truck to get here.' She checked her watch. 'I can't wait any longer. I'll have to leave the car here and call a taxi.'

'No need for that. You can take my car.' He handed her the keys, shaking his head when she started to protest. 'No, you need to fetch Charlie, that's the most important thing. Let's transfer his seat into the back of my car then you can get him while I wait here for the breakdown truck.'

He opened her car, quickly unclipping the seat belt so that he could remove the child seat. Hannah hurried ahead of him, opening the door so he could place it in the back of his car. 'I'll let you do the seat belt so you're sure it's fastened properly,' he explained, stepping aside.

Hannah fastened the seat into place then closed the door. She looked uncertainly up at him. 'Are you sure you don't mind, Tom? I mean, it's an expensive car and….'

'And nothing.' He placed his finger against her lips, feeling the tiny shudder that rippled along his veins when he felt the moistness of her breath on his skin. 'I wouldn't have offered if I hadn't wanted to. And a car is just a means of getting from A to B at the end of the day.'

She laughed softly, moving her head so that his hand fell to his side. 'Most men wouldn't agree with you about that. They see their car as an extension of themselves.'

'Everyone's different.' He shrugged, curbing the urge to find some other way to touch her. Even if he held her hand, it would be too much. 'Anyway, off you go and fetch the little chap. Don't bother coming back for me. Charlie's probably ready for his supper so I'll get the driver to drop me off at your house while I pick up my car.'

'But you could be here for ages,' she protested worriedly. 'I'll come back after I've fed Charlie.'

'No. You just worry about getting him settled. I'll be fine.' He smiled at her, loving the way her eyes had darkened with concern at the thought of him having to wait around. He couldn't remember the last time anyone had worried about him like this.

He blanked out the thought and shooed her into his car. The seat was too far back for her to reach the pedals so he showed her how to adjust it then closed the door. She waved as she drove away and he waved back, surprised at how lost he felt when the car disappeared round a bend. How would he feel when he left for Paris? he wondered as he settled down to wait for the breakdown truck. Bereft? Lost? Lonely?

He sighed. He would feel all those things and it just proved that the sooner he was gone the better.

It was almost eight p.m. by the time Hannah heard a vehicle pull up outside. She rushed to the window in time to see Tom climb out of the cab of the tow truck. Hurrying to the door, she swung it open, apology written all over her face.

'I am *so* sorry!' she exclaimed, ushering him

inside. 'I had no idea it would take the driver so long to get to you.'

'No worries.' Tom smiled at her as he stepped into the hallway. 'Apparently, it's been their busiest day this year. For some reason umpteen cars chose today to break down.'

'Typical,' Hannah snorted. She closed the front door and led the way into the sitting room. Picking up his keys from the old wooden trunk that doubled as both a toy box and a coffee table, she handed them to him. 'Anyway, I can't tell you how grateful I am for the loan of your car. It really was kind of you, Tom.'

'It was my pleasure.' He slid the keys into his pocket and looked around. 'I take it that Charlie's tucked up in bed?'

'He is. He wolfed down his supper, had his bath and that was it. I won't hear a peep out of him until the morning, I expect.'

'Obviously, you're a first-rate mum,' he said, laughing.

'Hmm, I don't think so. It's more a case of being lucky enough to have a child who sleeps.'

She shrugged. 'I'm still very much at the trial and error stage of motherhood, believe me.'

'I don't suppose anyone knows it all at first. It's a learning process, isn't it? That's what must make being a parent such a special experience.'

'You're right. It is special. I wouldn't swop being a mother for anything,' she admitted.

'I can see that.'

His eyes were tender as they rested on her and Hannah felt a rush of warmth pour through her veins. It had been a long time since she'd been on the receiving end of so much caring and it felt good. She turned away, not wanting to dwell on the thought that it was all the more special because it was Tom doing the caring. 'Can I get you a drink? Or some supper? You've been hanging around for hours waiting for that wretched truck—you must be starving.'

'No. It's fine. I'll get something at The Ship.' He glanced at his watch and grimaced. 'Although I'm cutting it rather fine. They stop serving at nine.'

'In that case, I insist. It's the least I can do after everything you've done for me.' She didn't give him time to protest any more as she hurried into the kitchen and opened the fridge. Taking out a packet of bacon and some plump local sausages, she placed them on the worktop. 'How about a fry-up? Sausage, bacon, eggs, mushrooms.'

'Sounds delicious. My mouth's watering already.'

He followed her into the room, sitting down at the table while she set to work. Hannah took her largest frying pan out of the cupboard and soon had the bacon and sausages sizzling away. She cracked a couple of eggs into the pan, scooping the hot fat over them to set the yolks before glancing up.

'A slice of fried bread to go with it? Or would that be overkill?'

'My cholesterol levels can stand it,' he assured her, taking off his jacket and draping it over the back of the chair. 'Just!'

'Good.' Hannah laughed as she placed everything onto kitchen paper to drain while she fried the bread. She added a slice for herself, unable to resist the delicious aroma wafting from the pan.

Tom groaned when she placed the loaded plate in front of him.

'If this tastes even half as good as it smells I shall be a very happy chappie.'

He dug in, wasting no time as he forked up a mouthful of food. Hannah put the kettle on then sat down opposite him and tucked into her fried bread with relish. 'I've no excuse for eating this,' she mumbled around a mouthful of the savoury concoction. 'I had supper with Charlie. *This* is pure greed!'

'A little of what you fancy does you good,' Tom teased her as he speared a mushroom with his fork.

'And puts inches on your hips,' she countered wryly.

'Rubbish! You certainly don't need to have any concerns on that score. You have a great figure, Hannah.'

She hadn't been fishing for compliments but that was how it must have sounded, she realised, and gave a little shrug. 'I've still got some of my baby weight to lose.'

'Well, you look great to me.' Tom picked up a piece of crispy bacon and offered it to her. 'How about some of this bacon? It really is delicious.'

'No, thanks. I refuse to let you lead me any further astray,' she retorted, then realised how that comment could be interpreted. Thankfully, either he didn't see it that way or judiciously chose to ignore the implication because he merely smiled as he bit the end off the bacon. He finished his supper in record time, leaning back in the chair with a sigh of contentment.

'That was great. It definitely made up for hanging around, waiting for that truck to arrive.'

'I'm glad. I don't feel quite so guilty now.' She removed their plates and took them over to the sink. 'What do you want to drink? Tea or coffee?'

'Oh, tea, please.' He stretched out his legs, trying to make himself comfortable on the hard-backed chair, and she frowned.

'Go on into the sitting room and I'll bring it through.'

'Thanks.'

He headed into the other room, opting for one

end of the sofa. Hannah made a pot of tea and loaded everything onto a tray, feeling a sudden attack of nerves assail her. It had been fine while she'd been busy cooking but all of a sudden she was acutely aware of the intimacy of the situation. After all, she and Tom were alone in the house apart from Charlie and she wasn't sure if that was a wise thing or not. Picking up the tray, she headed into the sitting room, determined that she wasn't going to be carried away by such foolish notions. Maybe they were alone but it didn't mean that anything was going to happen.

'How do you take your tea?' she asked, placing the tray on the trunk and kneeling on the floor next to it.

'Milk and two sugars, please.' He watched her pour the tea, nodding his head when she placed the mug in front of him. 'Thanks.'

Hannah poured some tea for herself, just adding milk. 'Obviously you're sweet enough,' he observed, and she grimaced.

'That's so old it's sprouted whiskers!'

He chuckled. 'Sorry. Obviously, I need to work on my chat-up lines.'

It was a throw-away comment and she knew that he hadn't intended it any other way; however, it had an effect all the same. Her hand was shaking as she picked up her mug and sat down.

'That was a slip of the tongue, Hannah,' he said quietly. 'I didn't mean to make you feel uncomfortable.'

'Of course not!' She gave a tinkly laugh as she lifted the mug to her mouth but the tea was too hot to drink so she put it down. 'Did the mechanic say how long it would be before my car's fixed?' she asked to change the subject.

'The garage will give you a call tomorrow and let you know. They may need to order a new radiator if they haven't got one in stock.'

'Let's hope they've got one in otherwise I'll have to hire a car. Is there anywhere local that hires out cars?'

'Jim Cairns will sort you out. He owns the garage and has a couple of vehicles that he hires out.'

'Oh, right. That's good to know.' She took a sip of her tea, wondering what else to say to keep the conversation flowing. It was easier while they were talking—there was less time to think. She searched her mind, finally settling on what had happened that afternoon. 'I hope the diabetic care team get Susan Allsop sorted out. She seems like a really nice person.'

'She is. Her husband is just the same, very easy to get on with,' Tom assured her.

'That's probably why they've made such a success of running their guest house.'

'I'm sure you're right.'

He picked up his cup, staring down at the tea with a concentration it didn't merit. Hannah bit her lip as she reached for her own cup. It was obvious that he was finding it as much of a strain as she was and just knowing that sent alarm scudding through her. She didn't want Tom to feel like she did. It was too dangerous.

She put down the cup, determined that she was going to keep control of the situation. 'I really appreciated you taking me with you today. It's given me a much better idea of where everything is.'

'Good.' His tone was flat. 'The worst part of starting a new job is finding your way around, I always find.'

'It is.' She summoned a smile. 'At least I won't get lost if I need to visit Dentons Cove again.'

'I hope not.' He took a swallow of his tea then put down the mug. 'That was great but it's time I was off.'

'Of course,' she concurred, hoping her relief wasn't too obvious. She jumped to her feet, only realising at the last second that Tom had done the same thing. They collided with a thud that knocked her off balance.

'Careful!' Tom caught her arm when she reeled back. He hauled her upright, his eyes very dark as he stared into her face. 'Are you OK?'

'I…um… Fine.'

Hannah heard the breathless note in her voice but there was nothing she could do about it. They were so close that she could feel the hardness of his chest against her breasts. Heat rushed through her when she felt her nipples tauten and realised that he must have felt what was happening to her too. There was a moment when he continued to stare into her eyes and then slowly, so very slowly that she wasn't sure if it was really happening, he bent and pressed his mouth to hers. That was when she knew it was real, when she felt his lips close over hers. Tom was kissing her, *really* kissing her, and although she knew it was foolish, she was kissing him back!

She heard him groan deep in his throat, heard him murmur her name in a tone that hinted at all the things he was feeling, from longing to despair, but it didn't surprise her. She knew how he felt because she felt the same way. She wanted this kiss and yet she knew in her heart it was wrong. It was just a question of which emotion would be the stronger, desire or common sense.

'This is crazy!' He tore his mouth away, cupping her face between his hands, and his eyes were filled with remorse as well as desire. 'I shouldn't be doing this. *You* shouldn't let me!'

'I know.' She met his eyes, knowing that he

would see the same conflict of emotions on her face. 'I know it's crazy. And I know that I'll regret it…'

'But?' he put in urgently.

'But I can't help myself,' she whispered. She raised her hands, holding his face between them as he held hers because she needed him to understand how powerless she was to stop what was happening. She wanted him and, despite all her reservations, nothing seemed to matter more than that. 'I want you, Tom. I want us to make love even though I know we shouldn't.'

'So do I!'

He pulled her back into his arms, holding her so close that she couldn't fail to feel the urgent power of his arousal pressing into her. His mouth was hot and hungry when it found hers again and she responded instantly to its demands. She kissed him with all the pent-up emotion that had been building inside her ever since they had met and felt the shudder that ran through him. That he should be so vulnerable shocked her because she hadn't expected that, hadn't expected a kiss to make him tremble like this.

A wave of tenderness rose up inside her as she pressed herself against him, letting him feel the effect he had on her. It was only fair that he should know how much the kiss had aroused her too. His arms tightened around her, moulding her against him in a way that left little to either of their imaginations. He could feel the hardness of her nipples pressing against his chest, she could feel his arousal…

He suddenly bent and swung her off her feet, lifting her in his arms as he walked towards the stairs. His face was set, his eyes dark pools of desire as he looked down into her face. 'Are you sure this is what you want, Hannah? Absolutely certain?'

'Yes,' she told him, because it would be a lie to say anything else. 'I want us to make love, Tom, even if we only do it this one time.'

She saw by his expression that he understood. This wasn't the start of something more. This was one night of passion, one night they could share; one night out of their lives that maybe… hopefully…they would look back on in the future with pleasure.

'It will be good,' he whispered as he kissed her hungrily. 'I'll make sure it is, Hannah, for both of us.'

'I know.'

She smiled up at him, not having any doubts about that. It would be good, better than that, it would wonderful because it was all they would have. One night out of all the thousands of nights to come. One night to enjoy each other's bodies, to let their passion soar, to feel things they would never feel again, at least not for each other. This one night was going to be so very special. It was going to be theirs.

# CHAPTER NINE

Tom didn't switch on the light as he carried Hannah into her bedroom. He didn't need to. He could enjoy her beautiful body just as much by touch and taste and feel.

A shiver ran through him as he laid her down on the bed. He had never envisaged this happening, actively tried to prevent it, but now they had reached this point he knew that he wouldn't regret it. No matter how hard it was in the future or how much he missed her, he would never wish that this night had never happened.

The thought filled him with tenderness as he bent and brushed her mouth with his. Her lips were so soft and sweet that he couldn't seem to get enough of them so the kiss ran on and on until they were both breathless. Drawing back, he stared into her face, loving the way that she didn't try to hide her feelings from him. Hannah had enjoyed the kiss as much as he had done and she was willing to own up to it too.

He sat down on the edge of the bed and gathered her into his arms, loving the feel of her body nestled against him. Sex for him in the past had always been a far more mechanical experience. He did this or that and achieved the desired results. However, he realised all of a sudden that this approach wasn't good enough tonight. He didn't want to add A to B and end up at C—no way! He wanted to be involved all the way through, wanted Hannah to be involved too. They weren't just having sex. They were making love.

The thought was so mind-blowing that he couldn't handle it. It opened up a whole host of possibilities he simply couldn't face. Dipping his head, he kissed her again, slowly and with a passion that seemed to spring from the very core of him, a place that had never been visited before. It was as though the feel of her mouth under his had opened up all the secret places inside him and the emotions he'd kept hidden there had come pouring out. If this was the difference between making love and having sex then it struck him how much he'd been missing.

His hand smoothed down her body, faithfully following the swell of her breasts, the dip of her waist, the curve of her hips. Although she was slender, she had curves in all the right places and he gloried in the feel and shape of her. His hand glided on, reached her thighs and lingered while he took a moment to breathe. It sounded crazy but his lungs didn't seem able to draw in enough oxygen any longer.

He breathed in greedily then groaned when he felt her nipples pressing against his chest. It would have taken a lot more willpower than he possessed to ignore their demand. His hand swept back up her body until it was cupping her left breast, the pad of his thumb sensually rubbing the hard, tight bud, and she sighed softly and with unconcealed pleasure. She turned slightly so that the full weight of her breast fell into his palm and he groaned again, unable to believe how good it felt to touch her. All his previous experiences suddenly paled into nothing and he realised with a jolt how ill equipped he was to handle this situation. Although he'd enjoyed his share of sex over the years and developed his skills as a lover, *making love* was very different. Although he knew that he could satisfy her physically, he wasn't sure that he could fulfil her emotional needs. Bearing in mind his earlier claims that this night was going to be special, he could only pray that he was up to it.

The thought made him tense and Hannah looked at him in concern. 'Tom? Is something wrong?'

'No,' he began, then realised that he couldn't lie. What if he failed to make this night as wonderful as he'd promised her it would be? He couldn't bear to think that he might disappoint her, that tomorrow morning she would regret what they'd done because it hadn't lived up to her expectations.

'I think I've got a bad case of cold feet,' he said, struggling to inject a little levity into his voice. It sounded closer to panic to his ears but he dredged up a smile in the hope that it would convince her.

'Cold feet?' She frowned. 'You mean that you don't want to go through with this…'

'No!'

The word shot out of his mouth and she jumped. She drew back, the frown that had been wrinkling her brow a moment earlier deepening. 'Then what do you mean?'

'That I'm scared stiff I'll disappoint you.' His voice was louder than he'd intended and he saw her glance towards the door. He moderated his tone, knowing that she was worried about him waking Charlie. 'Sex has always been just that in the past, Hannah, but this is different. I…well, I'm afraid that I won't be able to meet your expectations as I promised to do.'

'Oh, that's so silly!' The frown melted away as she leant forward and brushed her lips over his. 'You won't disappoint me, Tom. You'll see.'

He wasn't sure he shared her confidence but he wasn't going to labour the point. Not when she'd been so understanding. The tension oozed out of him, and he laughed softly as he gathered her into his arms. 'I hope you're right, sweetheart.'

'I know I am.'

Her lips found his, warm and soft and so achingly tender that his insides melted. However, when he tried to take charge of the kiss, she moved away, her mouth skimming across his cheek and along his jaw, her sharp little teeth nibbling the cord in his neck as it slid down his throat, and he shuddered. Never had he experienced anything quite so erotic as these hot, sweet kisses!

Her lips found the pulse at the base of his throat and stopped, the tip of her tongue snaking out to taste his skin, and he couldn't stand it any more. He needed to take a much more active role in the proceedings and to hell with worrying if he had the wherewithal to deliver on his promise! With one quick movement, he rolled her onto her back, using his forearms to support his weight as he loomed over her. Her eyes were huge, her lips parted, her breathing rapid, and his desire for her ran riot.

He kissed her hard and hungrily, not letting her go until the need to breathe became too urgent to ignore. They were both panting when he pulled back, both trembling, both filled with need, and his heart overflowed with all kinds of emotions when he realised it. Hannah wanted him just as much and in just as many ways as he wanted her!

The thought was all he needed. Dragging his shirt over his head, he tossed it onto the floor. Hannah was unfastening her blouse, murmuring in frustration when one of the tiny pearl buttons snagged on a loose thread. She undid it at last and tossed it aside, and he gulped. Although he hadn't switched on a lamp there was enough light filtering in from the landing to see by. The sight of her full breasts encased in that lacy white bra would have been temptation enough for any man. And it was way too much for him.

He slid the bra straps down her arms so that her breasts spilled out of their lacy covering. Her nipples were already dark and taut yet they tightened even more when he ran the palms of his hands over them. Hannah moaned softly and closed her eyes so he did it again, slowly and with exquisite care, feeling his own body respond in the most blatant way. Quite frankly, if he didn't get out his trousers soon he was in danger of doing himself permanent damage!

He shed his trousers and underwear then stripped off Hannah's skirt and panties. Her skin was smooth and warm to the touch when he ran his hands over it, flowing beneath his fingers like silk. He reached the very source of her heat and paused, wanting to be sure, one hundred per cent certain, that it was what she wanted. Even though it would be agony to stop now, he would do if it was what she wanted.

'Hannah?'

He didn't put the question into words, didn't need to because she understood. Opening her eyes, she looked at him and he felt a rush of relief run through him when he realised that there wasn't a trace of doubt in her gaze. Bending, he kissed her slowly and passionately, parting her lips as his fingers sought out her most secret place, and felt her shudder.

When he entered her a few moments later, Tom realised that nothing he'd experienced in the past had prepared him for this. This was what love-making was all about. This was how sex was meant to be. Here and now, with Hannah in his arms and their bodies joined in the most intimate way possible, he finally understood what he had been missing for all these years.

It was still dark when Hannah awoke, the sun not even peeping over the horizon. She lay quite still, listening to the sound of Tom's breathing while she tried to work out how she felt. Oh, she knew how she *should* feel—that was a given bearing in mind what had happened. But did she honestly regret making love with him? Did she wish it hadn't happened and feel angry with herself for giving in to temptation when she'd sworn she wouldn't?

A tiny sighed escaped her as she was forced to admit that she felt none of those things. She didn't regret their love-making, neither did she wish it hadn't happened. As for feeling angry with her-self, well, quite frankly, she felt more like leaping up and punching the air than anything else! Making love with Tom had been fantastic, better than that, it had been life-affirmingly wonderful from start to finish. The only thing she regretted was that she hadn't met him before she'd met Andrew and then the past miserable twelve months might never have happened.

A wave of euphoria washed over her and she wriggled a little, savouring the feeling, and heard Tom's breathing change. She forced herself to lie still in the hope that he would drop off back to sleep but it appeared the damage had been done. He rolled onto his side, pushing his hair out of his eyes as he peered at the dial of his watch.

'Five-fifteen? Do you always wake at this unearthly hour?' he murmured, his sleep-laden voice sounding sexier than ever, and Hannah couldn't stop herself. She wriggled again.

'Not normally,' she murmured, struggling to get a grip. So she and Tom had had great sex. Fine. Now it was the morning after the night before and although she'd be the first to admit that she wasn't an expert on the protocol of this kind of

situation, she suspected that she shouldn't make it quite so clear that she'd be happy if there was a repeat!

'So what woke you?' He lifted a strand of hair off her cheek and tucked it behind her ear and she did her best not to wriggle or tremble or anything else.

'I'm not sure. Maybe Charlie made a noise and it woke me,' she muttered, although it was an out-and-out lie.

'Hmm. Possibly.' His fingers traced the shell of her ear, following the curve until they reached her jaw where they lingered, warm and oddly reassuring, and she felt herself relax a little.

'Mother's instinct,' she claimed, happily perpetuating the small untruth because she enjoyed the feel of his fingers on her skin. 'We're programmed to wake at even the slightest noise our child makes.'

'So long as it was that and not the fact that you were worrying about what happened last night,' he murmured in a deceptively mild tone.

Hannah flushed, knowing that she'd been found out. 'That may have had something to do with it.'

'I'm sorry if you're upset, Hannah. It's the very last thing I wanted.' His tone was harsher now but it didn't disguise the underlying pain, and she knew that she couldn't allow him to jump to the wrong conclusions.

'I'm not upset.' She turned to face him. 'Last night was wonderful, Tom, and I enjoyed every second.'

'So did I.' He smiled but she could see the doubt in his eyes and knew that he still didn't understand. How could he when she'd had to work it out for herself?

'Good. It would be awful if you hadn't enjoyed it as much as me. And even worse if you regretted it.' Her eyes held his fast because she didn't want there to be any mistake about what she was saying. 'I don't regret what happened. Maybe I should, I don't know. After all, I don't make a habit of having one-night stands. But all I can say is that I enjoyed making love with you and that this morning I feel better than I've felt for a very long time.'

'Hannah! Sweetheart, I don't know what to say…'

He broke off, closing his eyes, and she guessed that he was struggling to get a grip on his emotions. The thought touched her deeply and she reached out and laid her hand on his cheek.

'You don't have to say anything. That's the beauty of this situation, isn't it? We spent the night together and enjoyed it. It's as simple as that.'

'Is it?' His eyes opened and she shivered when she found herself staring into their azure depths. 'Is it really that simple, Hannah?'

'It has to be. You're leaving in a few days' time and I'm staying here to build a new life for myself and Charlie. Last night was a one-off—we both knew that.'

'You're right. Of course you are.' He pulled her to him and kissed her lightly on the lips. 'I'm just glad that you're happy with the situation. I would have hated it if you'd been hurt or upset.'

He obviously meant that and her eyes filled with tears but she blinked them away. She wouldn't allow anything to spoil what they'd had, not when it had given her so much that she hadn't even realised she had lost. After they had found out that Charlie wouldn't be perfect when he was born, Andrew had become very distant. He had made no attempt to sleep with her, hadn't even shown any inclination to kiss or cuddle her. Although it had hurt to be rejected so thoroughly, she hadn't realised how much she had missed the physical contact until last night. Making love with Tom hadn't been merely a matter of them having great sex; it had been so much more than that.

The thought made her feel a little on edge but there was no time to worry about it when Tom's hands were stroking her body, bringing it to life once more. Maybe she should have stopped him by insisting that they had only agreed to the one night but it seemed churlish to do so, especially when she was enjoying his touch so much.

Hannah closed her eyes and gave herself up to the magic, feeling the hot waves of desire chase away all the hurt and loneliness she'd endured during the past year. When she was in Tom's arms, when his mouth was on hers and his hands were reminding her of how it felt to be a woman, she couldn't think about anything else. She didn't want to. She just wanted to enjoy what was happening and savour the time they had together.

One night may have turned into one night plus a morning but that was it. There wouldn't be any more. This was the last time they would make love, at least to each other, and she intended to appreciate every second, relish every minute. This was their time, hers and Tom's. A wonderful memory to look back on with pleasure.

'Ah, Tom. There you are. What happened to you last night, or shouldn't I ask?'

Tom felt a rush of heat invade him when he turned to find Simon standing behind him. Just for a moment his mind went blank, which was a miracle considering the thoughts that had been filling it on the drive to the surgery.

'Hmm. Obviously I shouldn't ask leading questions like that.' Simon laughed as he clapped him on the shoulder. 'Sorry. I didn't mean to pry. It's just that Ros mentioned your bed hadn't been slept in and we were worried in case something had happened to you.'

'I stayed with a friend,' Tom said, praying that his godfather wouldn't ask which friend. Out of the corner of his eye he saw the surgery door open and tensed when he saw Hannah coming in. She was wearing her usual working attire—a neat black skirt teamed with a crisp white blouse— but it was just the tiniest step back in time to picture what she'd been wearing the last time he'd seen her...

He blanked out the thought. Picturing Hannah naked in her bed wasn't going to help one little bit! Fortunately, Simon seemed to have been distracted by her arrival. He smiled jovially at her.

'Good morning, my dear. You're bright and early. I hope it isn't because you didn't sleep last night.'

'I...um...no, not at all.'

Tom saw the rush of colour run up her cheeks

and hastily intervened. Bearing in mind that it was his fault that she'd woken at such an unearthly hour, it seemed the least he could do. 'Did I tell you that I've managed to book myself on a flight to Paris leaving on Monday morning?'

'Good. Well, not good that you're leaving, of course, but I'm glad that you managed to get things sorted after all the recent shenanigans.' Simon sighed. 'Ros is still rather miffed because I said we couldn't go to see Becky but I really don't think it's fair to ask you to change your plans so late in the day. And it certainly isn't fair to Hannah to abandon her when she's only been here a week.'

Was that all it was? Tom thought wonderingly. They'd known each other not quite a week and yet it felt as though she'd been part of his life for ever.

'Maybe you can go later in the year,' Hannah suggested, and Tom knew—he just *knew*—that the same thought had flown through her head too.

He turned away, murmuring something about a patient needing an early blood test. It wasn't a lie. One of his patients was booked in for a fasting cholesterol test but Emily was doing it, not him. He made his way to the treatment room where he found Barry Rogers already waiting. He took the bloods, brushing aside Emily's apologies when she arrived a few minutes later and discovered it had been done. As he told her truthfully, she wasn't late, he was early and there was nothing to apologise for.

Tom made his way to his consulting room and busied himself with setting up for the day. It was a task that demanded minimal concentration but he focussed all his energy on getting ready. It was easier that way. Safer. He couldn't afford to let his mind wander, wouldn't allow himself to wish that he wasn't leaving. He had to leave to protect Hannah. Last night had proved that it would take very little for him to fall in love with her and that was something he couldn't countenance. Maybe he would love her for a short while but how long would his feelings last?

He'd thought he'd been in love with his ex-fiancée, hadn't he? After all, she had ticked all the boxes, at least on paper. She'd been beautiful,

witty, clever and sophisticated. He had enjoyed
spending time with her and had convinced himself that his feelings would last. He'd been determined to buck the trend and prove that he could
do what no one else in his family had done. He
was going to marry her and they would live happily ever after…only it hadn't worked out that
way. Just a few weeks after they'd announced
their engagement he'd started to have second
thoughts, and a couple of months further down
the line, he'd realised that he had made a huge
mistake.

Their break-up had been less than amicable,
not that he blamed her for that. After all, he was
the one who had changed his mind and she'd had
every right to be angry. But what if it happened
again? What if his feelings for Hannah melted
away as they had done before? She deserved so
much more after what had happened to her recently. She deserved to find happiness with a man
who would look after her for ever more. What
she didn't deserve was someone like him, some-

one who couldn't promise to love and honour her, and stick to it.

Tom stabbed his finger on the button to summon his first patient. He knew what he had to do and if it hurt then it was his hard luck. Far better to live with an aching heart than a guilty conscience.

# CHAPTER TEN

THE day proved to be less stressful than Hannah might have expected, given the circumstances. She spoke to Tom several times and there was no trace of awkwardness between them. Maybe it was the fact that they had set out clear boundaries before they had slept together but it was a relief, all the same. It made her feel very positive about what had happened. One of the worst things about her break-up with Andrew was the effect it had had on her confidence. However, last night had changed all that and she felt far more in control of her life.

She was on her way to the office after evening surgery finished when Simon waylaid her. 'I'm glad I caught you, my dear. I won't keep you because I know you must be anxious to collect your little boy from the nursery, but I just wanted to know if you're free on Saturday night. Ros is organising a bit of a "do" for Tom before he leaves. Everyone's coming—it's a proper staff outing, in fact, so naturally we're hoping you'll come along too.'

'I'm not sure if I can,' Hannah said slowly, wondering about the wisdom of what was being suggested. Last night may not have caused any major repercussions but would it be pushing it to spend another night in Tom's company? She hurried on, deciding that it would be silly to push her luck. 'I don't have a babysitter for Charlie, I'm afraid.'

'Oh, that's not a problem,' Simon assured her. 'Emily's in much the same boat as you. Her parents are away at the moment and she's not got a babysitter, so she's bringing her little boy along. There's no reason why you can't bring Charlie. I'm sure he'll enjoy it.'

'I'm sure he will,' Hannah murmured, realising that she couldn't refuse now. After all, she didn't want everyone to think that she was being stand-offish. And what on earth could happen, anyway? She and Tom were hardly going to be overcome by a fit of passion surrounded by their colleagues! She summoned a smile. 'In that case, I'd love to come. Thank you.'

'Wonderful! Ros will be delighted.'

Simon patted her on the shoulder then carried on. Hannah deposited her files in the tray then said goodnight to Lizzie and their part-time receptionist, Alison Blake. Emily came in as she was leaving and smiled at her.

'Simon just told me that you're going to bring Charlie on Saturday night.'

'That's right. I was a bit dubious at first but he told me you were bringing your son along too. How old is he?'

'Theo is two and a holy terror.' Emily laughed, her pretty face lighting up in a way that told how much she adored the little boy. 'He's into *everything*. Simon and Ros don't know what they're letting themselves in for!'

Hannah chuckled. 'From what Ros was telling me about their twins when they were small, I doubt they'll turn a hair.'

'Fingers crossed.' Emily grimaced. 'Anyway,

it will be nice to meet your little one. Hopefully he'll provide a distraction when my Theo gets into his stride!'

They both laughed before they parted company. Hannah got into the hire car that Jim Cairns had delivered to the surgery for her and drove to the nursery, thinking how good it was to have another woman in a similar situation to hers to talk to. She knew from various comments that had been made that Emily was a single mother too and it would be great to compare notes. The fact that Emily's son was not that much older than Charlie was an added bonus. It would be wonderful if the two boys grew up to be friends.

It was yet another positive thought and it helped to boost the feeling that her life was on the up at last. Maybe she hadn't envisaged sleeping with Tom but it hadn't had a detrimental effect, had it? And after the weekend it wouldn't be an issue. Tom would be on his way to Paris and that would be the end of the matter.

The thought should have buoyed her up even more but as she parked outside the nursery, she couldn't quell a pang of regret at the thought of not seeing him again. Maybe she had known him only for a week but there was no denying that he had made a big impression on her.

Tom spent the best part of Saturday packing. Although he travelled light there were always things that he accumulated along the way. He stored some of the books he'd bought in Simon's attic then put the remainder in a local charity's collection bag. Although his official home was the family's estate in Shropshire, he rarely went back there, so most of his belongings were scattered around the globe at the various places where he'd worked. At some point he would have to retrieve them, he thought as he added a couple of sweaters to the bag. However, before he did that he would need to have a place to take them. And having a home of his own wasn't something he had thought about. Until recently.

He sighed as he carried the bag out to his car. Getting hung up on the idea of setting down roots would be a mistake. Oh, he knew why he was thinking along those lines, of course. It was all down to Hannah. However, nothing was going to happen between them, at least, nothing more than already had.

Once again his thoughts flew back to that night they had spent together and he slammed the boot lid. He had to stop thinking about it! He had to stop torturing himself by wishing it would happen again. They had both agreed that it must be a one-off and he wasn't going to sink so low as to try to change her mind. When he left Bride's Bay, he intended to leave with a clear conscience.

Hannah put Charlie down for a nap at four o'clock then took advantage of the free time and had a bath. She washed her hair, wrapping it in a towel while she gave herself a much-needed pedicure. Looking after a baby as well as working left little time to pamper herself and it was a treat to indulge herself for once. She applied a coat of pale pink varnish to her toenails then blow-dried her hair, leaving it to fall around her face in loose chestnut waves. By the time Charlie woke up an hour later, she was ready. Putting an apron over the pretty floral dress she had decided to wear, she changed him into a clean blue T-shirt and matching shorts. With his dark curls all brushed and shining, he looked so adorable that her heart melted. How could anyone think that this gorgeous little boy was less than perfect?

She decided to walk to The Ship as it was such a lovely evening so popped Charlie in his pushchair and set off. She had just got there when Tom pulled into the car park so she waited for him because it would have been silly not to. He got out of the car, looking so big and handsome in a pair of well-washed jeans and a deep blue polo shirt that her heart melted a second time. If only Tom had been Charlie's father, she thought wistfully, then realised how foolish it was to think such a thing.

'Hi! That was good timing.' Tom came over to join them, stooping down so he could say hello to Charlie, who responded by holding up his arms to be picked up. Tom laughed as he lifted him out of the pram. 'Tired of being strapped in, are you, tiger? I don't blame you.'

He balanced the baby on his hip, making it look so natural that Hannah couldn't stop the previous thought resurfacing. Tom would make a wonderful father, a father who would love and care for his child no matter what. A lump came to her throat and she cleared her throat, afraid that her emotions would get the better of her.

'He hates being fastened in for long, which doesn't bode well for the evening. I only hope he doesn't disturb everyone when they're trying to enjoy their meal.'

'Nobody will mind,' Tom assured her. His eyes skimmed over her and he smiled. 'You look really lovely tonight, Hannah. That dress suits you.'

'Oh. Thank you.' She felt the heat rush up her face and turned away. He probably says that to all the women he's slept with, she told herself bluntly, but it had little effect. Maybe he did dish out compliments readily enough but there was no doubt that he had been sincere.

The thought was a boost to her ego. As she led the way into the pub, she couldn't help thinking how good it felt to be appreciated. Although

Andrew had taken a keen interest in her appearance, he'd been more concerned that she should look the part than anything else. He had wanted her to fit into the perfect life he'd been so eager to create for them and had expected her to dress accordingly. It struck her all of a sudden how empowering it was to be able to choose what *she* wanted to wear.

'Penny for them.'

Tom jogged her elbow and she jumped. She gave him a quick smile, unwilling to confess how influenced she'd been by her ex. She had been so eager to create that perfect life too that she had stopped being herself, and it was galling to admit it. 'Sorry, I was miles away. Shall I take Charlie?'

She held out her arms but Tom shook his head. 'No, he's fine with me, aren't you, sunshine?'

He brushed the baby's head with a kiss and once again Hannah was struck by how natural it looked. The fact that there was a definite similarity between him and Charlie also helped. As she followed him across the dining room, she couldn't help wondering how many people thought that they were a real family.

It was an unsettling thought mainly because she knew it would be too easy to get hung up on it. When they reached their party, she lifted Charlie out of Tom's arms and popped him in the high-chair that Ros had thoughtfully placed beside the table. Tom wasn't Charlie's dad and he never would be. There was no point fantasising.

'We're just waiting for Emily now and then we're all here,' Ros announced, beaming at them. 'Did you and Tom drive down together?'

'No. I walked,' Hannah explained, making sure the straps on the baby's harness were secure. She looked up and flushed when she saw the speculative look on Ros's face. It was obvious what the other woman was thinking and she hurried on. 'I bumped into Tom on the way in and he offered to carry Charlie.'

'It was perfect timing,' Tom said easily, pulling out a chair and sitting down next to the high-chair. He laughed when Charlie immediately made a grab for his nose. 'Oh, no, not the nose again, young man. If you keep on pulling it I'll end up like Cyrano de Bergerac!'

Everyone laughed. 'I take it that it's a favourite trick of his?' Ros said archly, and Tom grinned.

'Seems to be, doesn't it, Hannah? Every time I see this little chap, he makes a grab for my poor old nose.'

Hannah smiled, deeming it safer not to say anything. However, from the look on Ros's face, she was already adding two and two and coming up with her own answer! She busied herself with finding a bib for Charlie along with all the other paraphernalia he might need during the meal— wet wipes and a drinking cup, a plastic spoon and a dish. Tom studied the items she'd amassed with open amusement.

'It's like a military operation taking him out. You must have to be very organised.'

'You get used to it,' she assured him. She handed Charlie his cup of juice, her hand at the ready to catch it when he dropped it over the side of the chair, which he did.

Tom laughed out loud. 'You'd go down a storm on the local cricket team with reactions like that!'

'I get plenty of practice.' She smiled back, loving the way his eyes lit up when he looked at her. Maybe he was an accomplished flirt, but there was no point pretending that it didn't make her feel good to know that he found her attractive.

There was no time to dwell on that thought, thankfully, as Emily arrived just then. Once Emily and little Theo were settled, they decided to order. Hannah opted for chicken in lemon sauce, one of her favourite dishes. She'd brought a jar of baby food for Charlie and the waitress offered to warm it for her. It was brought back a few minutes later by a young man whom Tom introduced as Peter Granger, Barbara's son. Hannah smiled at him. 'It's nice to meet you, Peter.'

'You too, Dr Hannah,' he said shyly as he handed her the dish.

'Did your mum manage to arrange for you to visit the hospital?'

'Yes. I'm going next week to meet the doctors and nurses who'll be looking after me.' He gave her a quick smile. 'Mum says I won't feel so worried if I meet everyone before I have my operation.'

'It will be much nicer for you,' Hannah assured him.

'That was a good idea on your part, my dear,' Simon told her after Peter hurried away. 'Well done for thinking of it.'

'I can't take all the credit,' Hannah protested. 'It was Tom's idea. He'd seen the leaflet the hospital sent out and he showed it to me.'

'Excellent teamwork, then, wouldn't you say?'

Simon turned to Lizzie's husband and the subject was dropped. However, Hannah found herself thinking about the comment. She and Tom did work well together and there was no denying it. They seemed to be in accord when it came to their patients and there was no doubt at all that they were in even more accord in other areas.

Heat rushed through her and she busied herself spooning dinner into Charlie's mouth. She didn't want to think about how good it had been when she and Tom had made love. Maybe she would meet someone in the future who would make her feel just as good, but she would have to wait and see. She certainly wasn't going to rush into anything and end up regretting it.

If…and it was a very big *if*…she reached a point where she was ready to form another relationship then she would need to be sure it was not only right for her but right for Charlie too. Charlie had been let down once and she would never risk it happening again. *If* she did decide to spend her life with someone then he would have to accept Charlie for who he was. He would also need to love and care for Charlie as though he was his own flesh and blood because anything less wasn't acceptable.

It was a lot to ask of any man, Hannah thought, glancing at Tom. And especially of a man like Tom who'd admitted that he had problems with commitment. It made her see that wishing Tom could play a role in her and Charlie's future would be a mistake.

Tom had to admit that he had mixed feelings about the evening. Whilst he enjoyed being with everyone, it proved to be rather a strain to sit beside Hannah and pretend that they were nothing more than colleagues. Even though he knew it was how he must think of her, it was difficult after what had happened the other night. He kept getting flashbacks to the time they'd spent together, vividly erotic images of her laughing up at him, her lips swollen from his kisses, her eyes heavy with passion. And each time it happened, his nerves tightened that bit more and his body grew hot and hungry.

He wanted her again, wanted to make love to her, wanted to take her back to her house and do everything they'd done the other night, then wake up in the morning and do it all over again. It was like a hunger inside him, one he couldn't sate no matter how hard he tried to distract himself. It was a relief when everyone started to make a move. Emily was obviously eager to get Theo home, and Lizzie and her husband wanted to watch the latest episode of some reality show on TV. Tom smiled around the table, appreciating the fact that everyone had turned out to wish him well.

'I'd just like to thank you all for coming tonight. It's been a great evening and a great couple of months at the surgery too. I can honestly say that I've enjoyed every moment of my time here.'

'And we've enjoyed having you, Tom,' Simon assured him. He glanced at Ros and Tom frowned when he saw the look that passed between them. They were obviously up to something, although he had no idea what.

'I may as well cut to the chase, Tom. I've just received word that the primary care trust has decided to back plans to extend Bride's Bay Surgery. With several practices closing recently, they are concerned that there isn't sufficient provision for the number of patients in the area. Consequently Bride's Bay Surgery will be extended and given health-centre status. We'll have a full complement of staff—physios, midwives, community care nurses, etcetera. It also means that we'll need at least two more doctors.'

'I see,' Tom said slowly, suddenly realising

where this was leading. He cleared his throat. 'It all sounds very exciting.'

'It is.' Simon leant across the table. 'It's a wonderful opportunity not only for the patients but for the staff. That's why I want you to consider being part of it.'

'I don't know what to say,' Tom said truthfully. He glanced around the table, seeking inspiration. He didn't want to hurt Simon after everything his godfather had done for him but he knew that he had to turn down the offer. It went against his strictest rule to remain in one place for too long.

His gaze alighted on Hannah and he felt a rush of emotions hit him. Maybe it did go against everything he believed but surely rules could be broken if there was a good enough reason. If he stayed in Bride's Bay then he could get to know her better, allow these feelings he had to develop into something deeper. He could lie to himself all he liked but the truth was that she affected him in ways he had never imagined any woman could do. She made him long for a life he had always believed was beyond his reach. When he was with her he wanted it all—a wife, a family, a home of his own. But could he do it? Could he promise to be faithful and stick to it? Because one thing was certain: Hannah deserved nothing less than a lifetime's commitment.

# CHAPTER ELEVEN

THE party broke up a short time later. Hannah lifted Charlie out of the high chair and attempted to strap him into his pram but he was having none of it. He let out a loud wail, making it clear what he thought of the idea.

'It's all right, darling,' she said, soothingly. 'It'll only be for a few minutes so be a good boy for Mummy.'

She tried to settle him in his pushchair, no easy feat at the best of times thanks to the casts on his legs, but he resisted her efforts. She could see people turning to look and decided to give it up rather than disturb everyone. Hitching him onto her hip, she attempted to steer the pushchair towards the door, one-handed.

'Here. Let me take him.' Tom deftly lifted Charlie out of her arms and swung him into the air. He grinned when the little boy immediately stopped screaming. 'Hmm, it doesn't take much to cheer you up, does it?'

Hannah followed them across the restaurant, too relieved to have averted a scene to feel affronted that her son had responded better to Tom than he had to her. This wasn't the time to start having doubts about her ability as a mother!

Tom reached the door and waited for her, holding it open while she manoeuvred the pushchair outside. Lizzie and her husband Frank waved as they hurried over to their car. They were giving Alison a lift and the three of them soon disappeared. Emily and Theo had already left, and Simon and Ros had stopped to speak to Mitch Johnson. It meant that she and Tom were alone except for Charlie.

'Thanks.' Hannah summoned a smile, praying that Tom couldn't tell how on edge she felt. Simon's proposal that Tom should consider working at the surgery on a permanent basis had come like a bolt from the blue and she wasn't sure how she felt about it. Scared was probably the truthful answer, although there were other emotions trying to surface. Would she have slept with him if she'd had any idea this would happen? she wondered as they crossed the car park. Probably not, she decided, not when it could lead to all sorts of complications.

'Charlie's usually very good,' she said quickly, refusing to dwell on it. If Tom did decide to accept Simon's offer then she would have to deal with it. However, there was no point worrying unnecessarily, was there? 'But when he decides he doesn't want to do a thing then he really lets you know.'

'He's probably tired of sitting still, aren't you, sunshine?' Tom chucked the little boy under the chin, earning himself a sleepy smile. He settled him more comfortably against his chest then glanced at her. 'Shall I carry him home for you? There doesn't seem any point upsetting him again, does there?'

Hannah hesitated but she had to admit that it made sense. 'If you're sure you don't mind...'

'Of course I don't.'

There was a hint of impatience in his voice that surprised her, although she didn't say anything. It took them just a few minutes to walk back up the road from the harbour. It was still light, the sun riding low in the sky and casting a thick band of gold along the horizon. The fishermen were getting ready to set sail and the sound of their voices carried on the breeze. Hannah sighed as she reached for her key and unlocked the front door.

'It's so beautiful and peaceful here. I'd forgotten that places like this still exist.'

'Bride's Bay is very special,' Tom agreed, following her inside. He glanced at Charlie, frowning when he saw that the child's eyes were closed. 'I think he's asleep. Shall I carry him upstairs?'

'Please.'

Hannah moved aside, feeling her pulse leap when his shoulder brushed hers as he passed. She followed him up the stairs, reaching past him to open the door to Charlie's bedroom. It was little more than a box room, in all honesty, with a sloping ceiling at one end and a tiny window set in the eaves. However, the bright blue curtains and bedding printed with yellow diggers she'd chosen made it look very cheerful. Tom obviously thought so because he smiled as he looked around.

'I love this room. It's a real little boy's room. I wish I'd had a bedroom like this when I was growing up.'

'I had a lot of fun choosing everything,' she assured him. She took Charlie from him and laid him on the changing table, quickly changing his nappy and popping on a cotton sleepsuit. He didn't wake up as she gently placed him in his cot after she'd finished.

'Is that it?' Tom sounded so surprised that she laughed.

'Hopefully. I expect he's exhausted after all the excitement of being out tonight. With a bit of luck he'll sleep straight through till the morning.'

'You make it look so easy,' Tom said admiringly, following her from the room. 'So many people bang on and on about how hard it is looking after a baby, but you don't seem to have any problems.'

'Oh, I do, believe me. There've been days when I've been tearing my hair out. You just have to ride them out and hope things improve.'

'It can't be easy when you're on your own,' he said quietly, and she shrugged.

'It's just the way things are.'

She led the way down the stairs, not sure that she wanted to be drawn into a discussion about the difficulties of being a single parent. After all, it wasn't Tom's problem and it never would be. The thought was dispiriting and she hurried on. 'Well, thanks for walking us home. I really appreciate it.'

'Not a problem.' He gave her a quick smile. 'I'd better be off. There's still a few things I need to sort out ready for Monday.'

'Are you all packed?'

'More or less. I only ever travel light and that helps.'

'You can be up and off in a matter of hours,' she suggested, and he grimaced.

'Something like that.' He reached for the door latch then paused. 'I don't suppose I'll see you again before I leave, Hannah, so take care of yourself, won't you?'

'And you,' she murmured, feeling a sudden rush of tears spring to her eyes. She blinked them away but not fast enough obviously because he sighed.

'I hope those tears aren't for me, Hannah, because I don't deserve them. Whilst I don't regret the other night, I do know that I should never have allowed it to happen.'

'It wasn't down to you, though. It was what we both wanted.'

'Yes. And that means an awful lot to me, too.' He bent and kissed her on the cheek, his lips lingering in a way that told her how much he needed the contact. Maybe it was that thought or maybe it was the fact that all of a sudden she needed to touch him too but the next second her arms were around his neck. She heard him breathe in sharply and held on, sensing that he was about to pull away.

'Hannah, no. We mustn't. We agreed that the other night should be a one-off.'

The words should have brought her back down to earth with a bump. After all, what he said was perfectly true. However, no matter how sensible he was trying to be, it couldn't disguise the hunger in his voice.

'I know what we agreed, Tom. But can you put your hand on your heart and swear that you aren't tempted to spend one more night together?'

'I… No!'

He dragged her into his arms, holding her so tight that she was crushed against the wall of his chest. When he bent and kissed her with a hunger that he didn't attempt to disguise, she kissed him back, just as hungrily. Maybe they had planned on having only the one night but she needed this night too, needed Tom to hold her, love her, to turn her life into all positives.

He lifted her into his arms and carried her into the sitting room, laying her down on the sofa before kneeling down beside her. His eyes were tender as they skimmed her face, filled with a range of emotions that touched something deep inside her. Maybe he hadn't planned on this happening but it was what he wanted. She could tell that from looking at him and that was all she needed to know. He wouldn't regret them breaking the rules any more than she would!

'I've never met anyone like you, Hannah,' he said softly, cupping her cheek with his big warm hand.

'Haven't you?'

'No.' He pressed a kiss to her lips, drawing back so he could look into her eyes. 'Women have come and gone in my life and, if I'm honest, they've caused barely a ripple. But you're different.'

'There must have been someone special,' she suggested, wondering if he was spinning her a line.

'I thought there was once.' He sighed. 'I was engaged at one point but it didn't work out and we spilt up.'

'Is that why you avoid getting involved these

days?' she asked, feeling a small stab of pain pierce her heart at the thought.

'No.' He smiled as he brushed her mouth with a kiss. 'So if you think I'm suffering from a broken heart, forget it. I was the one who called things off. I realised that I'd lost interest and that going ahead with the marriage would be a huge mistake.'

'I see. And there's been nobody else since then?'

'Nobody important. Apart from you. I shall never forget you, Hannah.'

'I'm glad.' She kissed him on the mouth, more touched by the admission than she could say. Knowing that she meant something to him made what they had shared all the more special. 'I'll never forget you, either, Tom. You may not believe this but you've given me so much. And I don't just mean great sex!'

He laughed, his eyes filling with amusement. 'Is that a fact?'

'Hmm.' She smiled back, loving the fact that even in the throes of passion they could find something to laugh about. 'I'd lost a lot of my confidence in the past year but you've made me see that I can take charge of my life. I'll always be grateful to you for that.'

'And for the sex?' he suggested, leering comically at her.

'And for the sex,' she repeated, chuckling.

'Good.'

He dropped a kiss on her lips then let his mouth glide across her cheek and Hannah closed her eyes. She wanted to savour every second because this really would be the last time. His mouth glided on—along her jaw, down her throat, pausing when it came to the tiny pulse that was beating in such a frenzy of excitement.

'I love the way your pulse races when I do this,' he murmured. He pressed his mouth against the spot, the tip of his tongue tasting her flesh, and she shivered. Love-making, *Tom's way*, was so different from what she had experienced before. Even the smallest touch, the lightest caress, seemed to be so much more erotic. It felt as though she had never really made love properly before she'd made love with him and the thought was a revelation.

She twined her fingers through his hair, holding his head against her while he lavished more kisses on her throat. When his mouth moved on, she almost protested but there were more delights to come. His lips glided back and forth over the swell of her breasts, scattering kisses at random before finding her nipples and she gasped at the hot rush of sensation that rose inside her as he suckled her through the thin cotton fabric of her dress.

Her hands went to his back, stroking the long, strong line of his spine as she urged him to continue and he did. He drew back at last but only long enough to unzip her dress. He drew the bodice down, exposing her breasts in their lacy covering to his gaze, and she felt the shudder that passed through him and understood. If this felt like a first for her then it felt like that to him too.

'You're so beautiful, Hannah. So very, very beautiful.'

His voice was filled with awe as he ran his

palms over her throbbing nipples and she sighed. Like any woman who'd had a child, she was aware that her body had changed; however, any doubts she may have had about how she looked faded into nothing. Tom obviously liked what he saw and that was all she needed to know.

Closing her eyes, she gave herself up to the moment, letting the exquisite sensations grow and build inside her. When he eased the straps of her bra down her arms and took her nipples into his mouth one after the other, she cried out, unable to hold back the outpouring of emotion. Not even what had happened the first time they'd made love had prepared her for this!

Her hands went to the front of his shirt, wanting—*needing*—to feel him, skin on skin. Tom murmured something as he eased himself away and dragged his shirt over his head. He tossed it on the floor then lay down beside her, drawing her into his arms so their two bodies seemed to merge into one. Hannah bit her lip when she felt the warm, hair roughened skin on his chest brush against her aching nipples. Her senses seemed to be heightened to such a degree that it seemed almost too much to bear. It was the sweetest kind of torment to have to wait until their bodies were joined even more intimately.

'You make me wish things could be different, Hannah.' His voice was low, grating in a way that told her how much it cost him to make the admission.

'Maybe they can,' she said quietly, but he shook his head.

'No. No matter how much I may want to change, I daren't take that risk.' He took her face between his hands. 'I can't make you any promises when it could turn out that I'm incapable of keeping my word, like the rest of the Bradburys. All I can give you is this.'

He kissed her hungrily, his tongue mating with hers in a ritual as old as time. Hannah clung to him as she kissed him back, feeling the sharp sting of tears burning her eyes. Maybe it wasn't her place, but she wished with all her heart that she could make him see that he had the power to change if it was what he truly wanted. So what if he had called off his engagement because he'd lost interest in his fiancée? It didn't mean it would happen again. He set far too much store by his family's failings and failed to see that *he* could do whatever *he* wanted, but how could she make him understand that? Should she even try when it went way beyond what they had agreed?

Another night of passion was all this was. It wasn't the precursor to an affair, certainly wasn't the lead-up to anything more. It couldn't be. She needed to concentrate on building a new life for herself and Charlie. She didn't have the time for a relationship and all that it entailed. Maybe she would like to get to know Tom better. And maybe she would love to have the time to allow these feelings she had for him to develop but it wasn't going to happen.

It was the wrong time and the wrong place, and she knew that. As Tom drew her into his arms, Hannah realised that this was all she could ever have, these few hours in Tom's arms. It was up to her to make sure they were special for both of them.

* * *

Charles de Gaulle Airport was bustling when he arrived. Tom snaked his way between the crowds, thankful that he only had a carry-on bag and didn't need to wait for any luggage. The sooner he got to the clinic, the happier he'd be.

He sighed as he made his way to the car-hire desk. Leaving Bride's Bay that morning had been the hardest thing he had ever done. Right up until the moment his plane had taken off he had been tempted not to go through with it. He'd kept thinking about everything he was giving up—thinking about Hannah—and it had proved almost too much. It was only the thought of the harm it could cause if he stayed that had made him get on the plane.

Sadness washed over him as he realised that he could never go back. What had happened on Saturday night had proved beyond any doubt how vulnerable he was. Oh, he could try to justify his actions any way he chose but the truth was that he had wanted Hannah so much that he hadn't been able to stop himself making love to her. If he went back, it would happen again and again until he was completely under her spell… For however long it lasted.

It all came back to the same thing, he thought dully. He couldn't promise that his feelings would last. He could end up hurting her and he knew that he couldn't live with himself if he did that. No matter how painful it was, he had to make the break. The truth was that Hannah would be better off without him.

He handed the clerk his driving licence, waiting impatiently while she filled in the paperwork. She finally handed him the keys and he hurried outside to find the car. Five minutes later he was on his way to the start of a new episode in his life. That was how he must think of it, as a new beginning rather than the end of something special. He would focus on the future and whenever his mind tried to sneak in thoughts of Hannah he would stamp them out.

He took a deep breath. Give it a couple of weeks and he wouldn't remember what she looked like.

# CHAPTER TWELVE

THE days flew past and Hannah found herself increasingly busy. A steady influx of tourists into the town meant that their lists grew longer by the day. Both morning and evening surgeries were packed and usually overran. Although she worried about the amount of time she was away from Charlie, she was glad that there wasn't a minute to spare. At least while she was working, she wasn't thinking about Tom and that was something to be grateful for.

It was much harder when she was at home. Then her thoughts constantly returned to Tom. She kept wondering how he was and if he was enjoying his new job or if he missed Bride's Bay. Maybe he missed her too, missed the daily contact they'd had, missed hearing her voice as she missed hearing his. Even though she knew how silly it was, she hoped he did. Maybe Tom didn't *do* commitment, but she would hate to think that he had forgotten her. What they'd had together had been too special. It should be remembered.

She was in the office one lunchtime about three weeks after Tom had left, getting ready for the afternoon's anti-smoking clinic, when the phone rang. Lizzie had gone to the post office and Alison was tidying the waiting room so she picked up the receiver. 'Bride's Bay Surgery. Dr Morris speaking.'

She frowned when an unfamiliar voice asked to speak to Simon. Lizzie normally dealt with any phone calls, weeding out the ones from the various pharmaceutical companies that were keen to promote their products. She certainly didn't want to pass this on to Simon if it was yet another sales pitch.

'Who's calling, please?' she asked, deciding it would be simpler if she screened the call. Her frown deepened when the caller identified herself as the sister in charge of the IC unit at Christ Church hospital in New Zealand. She knew from what Simon and Ros had told her that that was where their daughter lived.

Hannah put through the call but she had a bad feeling about it. When Lizzie came back she quickly explained what had happened and could tell that she was concerned too. Abandoning her preparations, she went and knocked on the door of Simon's consulting room. He was sitting at his desk when she went in and she could tell at once that something awful had happened.

'What is it?' she demanded, hurrying into the room.

'That phone call. It was about Becky…' He broke off and she could tell that he was close to tears.

'Is she all right?'

'I don't know. There's been an accident. Becky and Steve were in their car when they were hit by a lorry. Steve…well, Steve's dead and Becky's in ICU.'

'How dreadful!' Hannah exclaimed. 'What about the baby?'

'She wasn't with them, mercifully. They'd left

her with a babysitter while they went out for dinner.' Simon stumbled to his feet. 'I'll have to tell Ros. Then we need to sort out what to do.'

He hurried out of the room, leaving Hannah at a loss to know what to do. Although she wanted to help, she knew that the couple needed time on their own to come to terms with what had happened. She went back to the office and told Lizzie what had gone on. Once Lizzie had recovered from her shock, Hannah asked her if she would contact everyone who was booked in for the clinic and explain that it had been cancelled. Simon was in no fit state to worry about work, so she would do the house calls then take over his list for evening surgery.

The sheer logistics of covering everything herself was mind-boggling but she refused to dwell on it. She collected the list of calls and set off. Thankfully, there weren't too many and she was back at the surgery shortly before three p.m. Simon came out to meet her as she drew up.

'Have you heard anything more about your daughter?' she asked as she got out of the car.

'She's been taken off life support and is breathing for herself,' he told her, his relief evident.

'That's good news.' Hannah followed him into the surgery. 'Have they said what injuries she's sustained?'

'A lot of internal damage, apparently.' He rubbed a hand over his eyes. 'I can't believe this has happened. As for Steve…well, what can I say? Becky's going to be devastated when she finds out.'

'She doesn't know yet?' Hannah said quietly.

'Not yet. In fact, they're thinking about holding off telling her until Ros and I get there in case the shock proves too much.'

'Have you managed to book your flight?'

'Yes. We leave tomorrow morning.' Simon sighed. 'Ros is packing. At least it's given her something to focus on. She was very fond of Steve—we both were. It's such a tragedy.' He made a valiant effort to rally himself. 'Anyway, about the surgery, I'm sorry to leave you in the lurch like this, Hannah.'

'Don't be silly. Nobody could have foretold

something like this would happen. I'll be fine. Really.'

'I know you will, especially now that I've arranged for Tom to give you a hand.' Simon smiled, mercifully missing the start she gave. 'I feel much happier now that he's agreed to cover for me. At least I won't feel that I have to rush back if he's here.'

'I...um...of course not.' Hannah managed a shaky smile, although she had never felt less like smiling. She quickly excused herself and went to her room, sitting down at her desk while she tried to deal with this new bombshell.

She had never imagined that she would see Tom again so soon. Whenever she'd pictured them meeting it had been at some point in the future. She'd assured herself that several months down the line she would be able to handle the encounter with equanimity. She would be polite but distant. And there certainly wouldn't be a repeat of what had happened the last time she'd seen him.

The pictures that were constantly hovering at the back of her mind came flooding back and she groaned. Would she be able to stick to that, though? Or would the temptation to spend another night with him prove too much? Tom had made it clear that he wasn't looking for commitment so could she handle a relationship that was based purely on physical attraction? She had no idea and that was the most worrying thought of all. She hated to think that the time might come when she wanted more than he could give her.

Tom pulled up in the surgery car park and switched off the engine. It was well past seven p.m. but the lights were still on. Leaving his bag in the car, he made his way inside, smiling at Lizzie who was looking uncharacteristically harassed.

'You're working late tonight. On overtime, are you?'

'Tom! Oh, it's so good to see you.' Lizzie rushed around the desk and hugged him.

Tom laughed as he hugged her back. 'I should go away more often if that's the sort of reception I get.'

'Don't joke about it.' Lizzie resumed her seat, grimacing as she glanced towards waiting room. Tom could see at least a dozen people still waiting and frowned.

'You are running late.'

'Tell me about it.' Lizzie rolled her eyes. 'It's been a madhouse here today. You wouldn't believe the number of folk who wanted an appointment. Poor Hannah has been run off her feet trying to deal with everything all on her own.'

'It can't have been easy for her,' Tom agreed, trying to control the flutter his stomach gave at the mention of Hannah's name. The butterflies that were flapping around inside him refused to settle down, however, and he gave up. He would save his energy until it was really needed, like when he actually saw her.

The thought sent a rush of blood to his head as well as to other parts of his body and he cleared his throat. 'I may as well see some patients while I'm here. Give me a couple of minutes to get set up then send the next one through, will you?'

'It'll be a pleasure!' Lizzie grinned as she

handed him a buff folder. 'Mrs Price has been moaning on and on about the length of time she's had to wait so I'll let you deal with her. A dose of the legendary Bradbury charm should work wonders!'

'Thanks. I think!' Tom replied drolly, although the comment had touched a nerve. Even Lizzie saw him as somewhat lightweight, the sort of man who charmed his way out of awkward situations.

The idea wouldn't have fazed him normally. However, as he made his way to the consulting room, he found himself regretting the fact that he had earned himself that kind of a reputation. He didn't want to be thought of merely as a charmer but as someone who could be relied on and it wasn't the first time he had thought that either if he was honest. In the past few weeks, he'd realised that his attitude to life had changed. Although he had always given one hundred per cent when it came to his work, it no longer seemed enough that he should deal with a patient and send them on their way. He wanted to be involved, long

term, to see their treatment through to its con-
clusion, and that was something that had never
bothered him before.

Was it meeting Hannah that had made the difference? he wondered as he switched on the lights.
His outlook on life had altered because he felt so
differently about her? He guessed it was true and
it was worrying to know how big an influence
she'd had on him. Although he hadn't hesitated
when Simon had asked for his help, he had realised what a risk he was taking by returning to
Bride's Bay.

He had tried his best not to think about Hannah in the past few weeks, but he hadn't succeeded. She'd got so far under his skin that he
could no more forget about her than he could forget about breathing. It made him see how careful
he would have to be. It would be far too easy to
allow his feelings to dictate his actions and that
was something he couldn't afford to do. Maybe
he had changed in a lot of ways but it didn't mean
that he was capable of making a commitment and
sticking to it.

* * *

Hannah checked her watch. Although she had phoned the nursery to warn them she would be late, she'd never imagined it would take this long to get through the list. She got up and hurried out to the corridor. Hopefully, Lizzie could reschedule some appointments for the morning. Even though it would mean her coming in extra early, it would be better than leaving Charlie any longer.

'Hello, Hannah. How are you?'

The sound of Tom's voice brought her to a halt. Hannah turned round, feeling her pulse leap when she saw him. He gave her a tight smile and she could see the wariness in his eyes. Was he thinking about that last night they'd spent together, regretting the fact that it had happened? It was impossible to tell so she could only speculate, based on her own feelings. Whilst she didn't regret sleeping with him, she did regret the fact that she'd not been able to put him out of her mind ever since.

'Tom. I wasn't expecting you till tomorrow.'

'I noticed that the lights were on when I arrived

so I called in.' He shrugged. 'I thought I'd give you a hand, seeing as I was here.'

'That was good of you,' she said stiffly.

'Not at all. I'm happy to help.' He glanced at his watch and frowned. 'What's happening about Charlie? You normally pick him up before now.'

'I phoned the nursery and warned them I'd be late, although I didn't expect to be this late,' Hannah admitted, worriedly. 'I'm hoping that Lizzie might be able to persuade a few people to rebook their appointments for the morning.'

'Don't worry about that. I'll see them.' He shook his head when she started to protest. 'No, I mean it, Hannah. You get yourself off and collect Charlie. That's far more important.'

'Well, if you're sure...'

'I'm sure.' He smiled at her and she couldn't stop her heart leaping when she saw the warmth in his eyes. 'Go on—off you go. Charlie must be wondering where you've got to.'

'I'm sure he is.' Hannah smiled back, unable to keep the warmth out of her eyes too. 'It's good to have you back, Tom.'

'It's good to be back,' he said softly, and she could tell that he meant it.

Hannah hurriedly fetched her bag, trying not to speculate about what it could mean. Tom had stressed how reluctant he was to remain in one place for any length of time, yet he seemed to be genuinely pleased to be back in Bride's Bay. Had he had a change of heart? Was he now prepared to consider settling down? She had no idea but the thought buoyed her up. The idea of Tom becoming a permanent fixture in her life was far more attractive than it should have been.

Tom saw the rest of the patients then sent Lizzie home and locked up. He set the alarm then made his way through to the house. It felt odd not to have Ros there to greet him, he thought as he switched on the lights. Normally she would have supper ready and they would eat it sitting around the kitchen table while they swapped stories about their day.

It was one of the things he enjoyed most about being in Bride's Bay, in fact. Normally he ate out, dining at various expensive restaurants wherever he happened to be living at the time. Although the food was always excellent, he much preferred the casual intimacy that came from sharing a meal with people he liked. He couldn't help thinking how good it would be if he had someone to go home to on a permanent basis, someone like Hannah, for instance. He could imagine how much better his evenings would be if he could spend them with her.

He sighed as he filled the kettle and switched it on. He mustn't think like that, mustn't let himself be seduced by the thought of a life with Hannah. The idea of domestic bliss might seem attractive at the moment but would it still appear so in a few months' time? It wasn't fair to Hannah to start something he might not be able to continue, neither was it fair to Charlie. He had to stop daydreaming and accept his life for what it was. He had a lot to be grateful for, after all. He was single, healthy and unencumbered by responsibilities. He could go wherever he chose and do whatever he wanted. A lot of men would give their right arms to be in his position.

Tom made himself a cup of coffee and took it through to the sitting room. He switched on the television because it seemed far too quiet with only himself for company. And if his thoughts wandered more than once to Hannah, he told himself it was only to be expected. After all, he cared about her and Charlie, and hoped they could be friends, although he understood if she preferred to keep her distance. He'd only be in Bride's Bay until Simon got back and then he'd move on, maybe return to Paris or go somewhere else. The world was his oyster, as the saying went. He could go wherever he wanted…

Except the only place he *really* wanted to be was right here.

In Bride's Bay.

And with Hannah and little Charlie by his side. Oh, hell!

# CHAPTER THIRTEEN

HANNAH felt exhausted when she arrived at the surgery the following morning. Unusually for him, Charlie had been difficult to settle the previous night, clinging to her and sobbing when she had tried to put him in his cot. She'd ended up sitting in the rocking chair with him until he had dropped off to sleep. He'd woken several times during the night too and each time she'd had to go through the same routine. She guessed that it might have had something to do with her having been so late collecting him from the nursery and could only hope it wouldn't happen again. She'd be in no fit state to work if she lost another night's sleep.

'Good morning. How are you today?'

'Tired.' Hannah summoned a smile as she turned to greet Tom. She felt a shiver run through her when she saw that his hair was still damp from his morning shower. She knew from experience that it would feel cool and silky to the touch and swallowed a groan. She really didn't need this today of all days!

'Rough night?' he asked, frowning.

'You could say that. Charlie woke up several times and I couldn't settle him.'

'That's not like him. Is he sickening for something?'

He sounded so concerned that her heart melted and she smiled at him. 'I think it had more to do with the fact that his routine had been disturbed.'

'Because you were late collecting him from the nursery?' Tom sighed. 'It's not fair to you or Charlie, Hannah. We'll have to make sure you leave on time from now on.'

'Easier said than done,' she said lightly, because it would be far too easy to wallow in his solicitude. 'If it continues to be as busy as it's been lately then we'll need to extend our opening hours, not reduce them.'

'It certainly proves that Simon's right about this

new health centre. Obviously, there's an urgent need for it.'

'There is. Even without the addition of any visitors to the town, we're hard pressed to cope.' She paused, wondering if she should ask the question, but in the end it was too tempting to resist. 'Have you thought any more about what Simon suggested?'

'That I should consider joining the team?' He shrugged. 'I don't think so. I can't really see myself spending the next twenty-odd years working here.'

Lizzie popped her head round the office door just then to say there was a phone call for him so Hannah was spared having to find anything to say. However, as she made her way to her room, she could feel her spirits sinking. Nothing was going to induce Tom to stay in Bride's Bay. It made her see how foolish it would be to harbour any hope that he might have changed his mind. He was a free agent and he obviously had every intention of staying that way.

The morning flew past. With appointments

scheduled every six minutes, Tom was hard pressed to keep up. Six minutes wasn't long enough to take a history and make a diagnosis and he refused to cut corners. By the time he came to his last patient, he had given up all hope of sticking to the schedule.

The sooner this new health centre was built the better, he thought as he pressed the buzzer. There was obviously a need for it plus it would give the community access to a lot more facilities. It was an exciting prospect, in fact, and he found himself wishing all of a sudden that he could be part of it, before common sense reasserted itself. He wasn't going to stay around long enough to play a role in the new centre's inception.

The thought was more dispiriting than it should have been. He pushed it aside as Mitch Johnson entered the room. 'Morning, Mitch. What can I do for you today? It's not your blood pressure, is it?'

'No, no, that's fine. I saw Emily last week and she was quite happy with the reading,' the landlord of The Ship informed him. 'Going back onto my usual medication has settled things down nicely.'

'Good. I'm glad to hear it.'

'Did you ever manage to speak to that locum at the hospital who changed my tablets?' Mitch asked as he sat down.

'Yes, I did. He said that he'd prescribed them for other patients and they'd had a beneficial effect.' Tom shrugged. 'What suits one person doesn't always suit another is all I can say.'

'I suppose so. Anyway, I'm here about this cough I have. It's been going on for weeks now and it's driving me mad. I've tried all sorts of cough medicines from the chemist's but they've not done any good.'

'What sort of a cough is it? Dry or chesty?'

'A really dry one, and it's worse at night, too. Marie said that if I don't do something about it, she's going to divorce me. She's fed up with me waking her up every night, coughing!'

Tom laughed. 'Well, we can't have that. Let me listen to your chest and see if we can find out what's causing it.'

He picked up his stethoscope and listened to Mitch's chest, back and front. 'Your chest's clear, which is what I expected. The kind of dry cough you described is usually associated with asthma, an infection or even an allergic reaction.'

'I've never suffered from asthma,' Mitch protested.

'No, I know that. You'd have other symptoms if you did, like breathlessness and wheezing. It could be that you've picked up a bug. Have you had a temperature or felt under the weather?'

'No. Apart from this cough I feel fine.' Mitch rolled his eyes. 'I was coughing so much this morning that the blasted parrot started copying me!'

'Parrot? I didn't know you had a parrot,' Tom said, frowning.

'It was Marie's idea. She had one when she was a child and decided that we should have one at the pub. I wasn't keen but you know what she's like when she gets an idea in her head—there's no stopping her.'

'So when did you get it?'

'Oh, it must be almost a month ago now.'

'And how long after it arrived did this cough start?'

'A week, maybe a bit less…' Mitch broke off and stared at him. 'You think Polly could be the cause of me coughing?'

'I think it's a distinct possibility. A lot of people are allergic to birds' feathers. You could be one of them.' Tom grinned. 'It could come down to a straight choice if I'm right—you or Polly. One of you may have to go.'

'And I know which one Marie will choose in her present state of mind,' Mitch replied gloomily.

He took the script Tom handed him and left, promising to come back if the cough hadn't cleared up in a week's time. Tom was still smiling as he gathered up the notes and took them through to the office. He could just imagine feisty Marie's reaction if Mitch suggested her beloved bird would have to go!

'Good morning?'

He glanced round when Hannah came in, trying to quell the lurch his heart gave. It didn't matter that it was only a couple of hours since he'd seen her, he still found himself reacting to the sight of her. 'A busy one. I'm way behind schedule.'

'Me too.' She sighed. 'Six minutes for each appointment isn't long enough, is it?'

'No, it isn't. Simon used to allow at least ten minutes for each patient, and even then some needed a lot longer than that.'

'I know. The trouble is that there's so many people wanting appointments these days that we'd never get through the list. Reducing the time allocated to each patient is the only way we can fit everyone in.'

'But it doesn't work,' he pointed out. 'We've both run over time this morning and no doubt we'll do the same again tonight. The only way to solve the problem is by hiring another doctor.'

'That's not something we can do, though. Simon's the only one who can make a decision like that.'

'Unfortunately, he is.' Tom shook his head. 'And he's got enough on his plate without having to worry about taking on additional staff. But once he gets back, I'm definitely going to suggest it to him.'

'It's not really your problem, though, is it? Or it won't be once Simon gets back.'

'Because I'll be leaving?' He shrugged. 'Maybe not, but I don't like to think of you two struggling even if it doesn't directly affect me.'

Hannah didn't say anything, leaving him with the impression that she didn't believe his concern was genuine and it was galling to know she thought that. As he made his way through to the house to make himself some lunch, Tom found himself wondering how he could convince her that he really did care...

He sighed when it struck him that it was the last thing he should do. Letting Hannah know how important she was to him would be a mistake. He needed to keep his distance, for her sake as well as his.

The week came to an end much to Hannah's relief. Whether it was the fact that they had continued to be so busy at the surgery or because Charlie had kept waking up at night, she didn't know, but she felt worn out. She got up on Saturday morning, gave Charlie his breakfast and dressed him. Leaving him playing with some building blocks, she had a shower and got dressed, opting for a pair of white linen trousers and a sleeveless cotton top. It was a glorious day, the sun beating down from a cloudless blue sky. She was sorely tempted to spend the day in the garden but there were jobs that needed doing, the first one being a long overdue trip to the supermarket.

She carried Charlie out to the car and strapped him in his seat. It was already hot outside and she turned on the air conditioning. There was a queue of traffic heading for the retail park so it was slow going and Charlie was grumbling by the time they arrived. Hannah carried him over to where the trolleys were parked, but the moment she tried to put him into the baby seat, he started squirming around.

'Come on, darling, be a good boy,' she said persuasively. 'Once we've done the shopping, we'll go home and play.'

She managed to settle him in the seat and fastened the harness. The supermarket was packed and it seemed to take twice as long as normal to get round all the aisles. By the time she joined the queue for the checkout, Charlie had had enough and started wailing loudly.

Hannah found his cup of juice in her bag and tried to pacify him with that but he refused to drink it and cried all the harder. He was making such a racket that people were turning to see what was going on. She was just about to abandon her trolley and leave when Tom appeared.

'Hey, what's all that noise about, young man?' He bent and blew a raspberry on the back of Charlie's hand. The little boy immediately stopped crying and looked at him in surprise. Tom grinned as he blew a second raspberry on the baby's cheek and was rewarded by a chuckle. 'That's better.' He straightened up, the smile still lingering as he turned to her. 'I take it that he's tired of being in the trolley.'

'That, plus the fact that he's due for his morning nap,' Hannah explained. She took a quick breath, determined that Tom's unexpected appearance wasn't going to throw her. 'I didn't expect it to be so busy.'

'There's a sailing regatta on today so I expect a lot of people have come to watch that.' He held up his basket. 'I'm going to watch it myself and came to buy a few bits and pieces to make a picnic.'

Hannah's brows rose as she studied the contents of his basket. 'Smoked salmon, pâté, oysters, Champagne…not quite your usual picnic fare.'

'You mean it should have been curling cheese sandwiches and stewed tea out of a flask?' He grinned at her. 'Pass! I think I can do a bit better than that.'

'It looks like it, too.' Hannah laughed, appreciating the fact that he'd taken her teasing in good part. She glanced round in relief when the queue started to move. 'Thank heavens. We might get out of here before teatime.'

'With a bit of luck.' Tom bent and tickled Charlie under the chin when the little boy began to fuss again. 'You can't wait to get out of that trolley, can you, tiger?'

'He hates being fastened in,' Hannah explained. She broke off a grape and popped it in the baby's mouth in the hope it would distract him but he spat it out.

'Why don't you take him outside while I pay for your shopping?' Tom suggested.

'Oh, I can't let you do that!'

'Why not? I need to pay for my shopping, so it's not a big deal to pay for yours as well. And surely it's easier if I queue up instead of keeping poor Charlie here any longer.'

'But I don't have enough cash on me to pay for all this,' Hannah pointed out. 'I was going to use my debit card.'

'You can pay me back next week. I'll trust you not to flee the country,' he told her, grinning.

Hannah laughed. 'OK. You've talked me into it, not that I took much persuading.' She lifted Charlie out of the seat. 'I'm parked over on the far side of the car park, near the railings.'

'I know. I parked next to you,' he informed her,

taking charge of her trolley. The queue moved forward again and he sketched her a wave. 'See you later.'

'Thanks, Tom,' she said quietly, and he turned and smiled at her.

'You're welcome. I'm happy to help any way I can.'

He pushed the trolley towards the checkout as she made her way from the queue. Charlie was gurgling happily now that he'd been freed from the seat, bouncing up and down as he pointed to things that caught his eye. Hannah responded automatically as they made their way out of the store. There'd been something in Tom's voice when he'd said that he was happy to help, which told her it hadn't been just the usual sort of meaningless remark people made. He'd genuinely meant it and it was good to know that he cared enough to want to make her life easier.

She sighed as she carried Charlie over to a patch of grass near to where she'd parked and put him down. She was looking for signs that Tom felt something for her and it was pointless. Maybe he *did* care and maybe he *did* want to help, but he wasn't about to change his whole way of life for her, and why should he? She was a single mum with a small child who would need a great deal of care in the coming years. Maybe they were compatible, sexually, but that wasn't enough to make him want to spend his life with her, was it? The most they could ever be was friends and she should be happy with that.

Hannah knelt down on the grass, trying not to think about what she really wanted. She had to focus on what really mattered, on making sure that Charlie was healthy and happy. If she achieved that aim then she would be perfectly content.

Tom paid for the groceries and wheeled the trolley out of the store. He crossed the car park and stopped beside Hannah's car. There was no sign of her and Charlie and he looked around, quickly spotting them sitting on the grass.

His heart lifted as he saw little Charlie laugh when Hannah tickled him. It was lovely to see them having so much fun together, he thought. It struck him all of a sudden how much he had missed being part of both their lives while he'd been in Paris. He had missed Hannah, of course, but he had also missed Charlie too, and that surprised him. He hadn't realised how fond he'd grown of the little boy or how much he'd enjoyed being around him. It made him reassess his ideas on fatherhood. Maybe he shouldn't rule out the idea of having a family of his own one day?

It was something Tom knew he needed to think about but not right now. Leaving the trolley next to the car, he went over to them. 'If you let me have your keys, I'll load your shopping into the boot.'

'Are you sure you don't mind?' Hannah said, hunting her keys out of her bag.

'Of course not.' Tom took the keys off her. 'I won't be long.'

He went back to the cars and sorted out the groceries, putting his shopping into his car once he'd dealt with hers. Hannah smiled when he went back a few minutes later.

'That was quick. It takes me a lot longer than that to sort everything out.'

'What can I say?' He blew on his knuckles and polished them on the front of his T-shirt. 'Talent will out.'

'So they say.' She laughed as she attempted to stand up, no easy feat with Charlie in her arms.

Tom put his hand under her elbow to help her, feeling the hot surge of blood that scorched his veins when his fingers encountered warm, bare flesh. Although her outfit was in no way revealing, it was very different from her usual attire, and he found his senses suddenly going into overdrive as he took stock of the way the cotton top clung to the lush curve of her breasts.

'Thanks.'

Hannah hastily stepped away and he realised that he wasn't the only one who'd been affected by his touch. Had she felt it too, he wondered, felt the blood rush through her veins, leaving her feeling breathless and giddy like he was?

'Well, I suppose I'd better get off home before the fish fingers start to defrost.' She gave him a quick smile but he could see the awareness in her eyes and had his answer. She was as receptive to his touch as he was to touching her and the realisation drove every sensible thought from his head.

'What are you doing this afternoon?' he said hurriedly as she started to move away.

She stopped and glanced back. 'This afternoon?'

'Yes. Have you anything planned?'

'Oh, just the usual.' She shrugged when he looked at her. 'You know—washing, ironing, cleaning—all the jobs I don't seem to have time for during the week.'

'But there's nothing really urgent on the agenda, though?'

'No, I suppose not,' she conceded.

'In that case, can I persuade you to put off doing them for a while longer?'

'Why?' she demanded bluntly.

'Because I'm hoping that you'll agree to spend the afternoon with me, you and Charlie, I mean.' He took a deep breath, wondering if he was mad to suggest it. 'We can go to Dentons Cove and watch the regatta. Charlie will love seeing all the yachts. And when he gets tired of that, I can show him how to make sand pies...' He tailed off when she shook her head.

'I don't think it's a good idea, Tom.'

'Why not?' he demanded belligerently, because he really, really wanted her to agree.

'You know why.' She tipped back her head and looked him in the eyes. 'I have no intention of sleeping with you again.'

'I never asked you to!'

'No, you didn't. But we both know it will happen if we spend any time together. It's happened twice already and I don't intend for it to happen a third time.' She gave a little sigh. 'I'm sorry, Tom, but I think it would be better if we stuck to being colleagues. It's simpler that way.'

'If that's what you want,' he said, shocked by how shattered he felt. Even though he knew it made sense, it hurt to be rejected.

'It is.'

She gave him a quick smile then walked over to

her car. Tom stayed where he was and watched as she strapped Charlie into his seat and drove away. He was tempted to go after her but what was the point? She wouldn't change her mind and why should she? All he'd ever offered her was sex and although it may have been the best sex he'd ever had, it wasn't enough for someone like Hannah. She deserved so much more, a lifetime's worth of commitment at the very least, and he couldn't give her that.

Could he?

The question seemed to sear itself into his brain. As he got in his car, Tom could feel it burning deeper and deeper into his psyche. Could he commit himself to Hannah and mean it? Could he promise to love her for ever and stick to it? A couple of months ago he would have scoffed at the idea of him remaining true to any woman, but now it didn't seem such an alien concept. Not if that woman was Hannah.

# CHAPTER FOURTEEN

THE next couple of weeks passed in a blur. Hannah felt as though time was moving at twice its normal speed. The fact that it continued to be so busy at the surgery didn't help either. Both morning and evening surgeries were packed and finishing on time was a pipe dream. Although Tom offered several times to see some of her patients so she could go and collect Charlie, she always refused. It just seemed better that she maintain her independence.

As for Charlie, he was still waking up at night. His casts had been removed and he'd been given special boots to wear. Made from a soft material, with a metal bar to keep his feet at shoulder width apart, he had quickly learned to cope with them during the day. However, they needed to be worn at night too and he hated having them put on after his bath. Hannah tried everything she could think of to distract him, playing umpteen games of peek-a-boo and singing to him, but as soon as he saw her pick up the boots, he started screaming and it took her ages to calm him down. Between the stress of that and the situation with Tom, it was little wonder her nerves felt as though they were in shreds.

On a more positive note, Simon's daughter was making excellent progress. She had been discharged from hospital and Ros was looking after her. Simon phoned several times to update them on her progress and Hannah wasn't surprised when he started talking about coming back to England. The plan was that Ros would stay in New Zealand to look after Becky and the baby while he returned. Although she would be glad to have him back, it meant the time was fast approaching when Tom would leave. Even though she knew it was for the best, she couldn't help feeling lost at the thought of never seeing him again. Several times she even found herself wishing that she'd agreed to go on that picnic with him. At least it would have been another memory, something else to look back on in the future.

She had just finished the weekly antenatal clinic when Lizzie popped her head round the door. Tom was doing the house calls and she assumed he'd phoned to warn them he would be late for evening surgery. It had happened a couple of times and she sighed at the thought of yet another late finish.

'Has Tom phoned to say he's going to be late?' she asked, piling some leaflets on healthy eating into a cardboard box.

'No. Jim Cairns is on the phone,' Lizzie explained. 'A man has fallen down the cliffs roughly halfway between here and Dentons Cove. The lifeboat's on standby in case he goes into the sea but, apparently, he's stuck on a ledge. The search and rescue team are on their way but they don't have a doctor with them. Jim wants to know if you or Tom can help.'

'Of course,' Hannah agreed immediately. Leaving the rest of the leaflets on the desk, she picked up her bag and checked the contents. 'I could do with some more saline… Oh, and some morphine as well.'

'I'll ask Emily if she can get them for you,' Lizzie offered.

Emily arrived a few minutes later and handed Hannah the items she'd requested. 'Lizzie said that someone has fallen off the cliff.'

'That's right.' Hannah frowned as she mentally ran through a list of what she would need. 'Will the search and rescue team have things like splints and bandages?'

'Oh, yes. They're very well equipped,' Emily assured her, following her from the room. 'These things can take quite a bit of time so if you get stuck, call me. I can pick Charlie up from nursery when I collect Theo. He knows me quite well now so he should be all right about it, especially as Theo will be with me. They play together, I believe.'

'Would you?' Hannah smiled in relief. 'Thanks, Emily. I'll phone the nursery and let them know what's happening if it looks like things are going to drag on.'

She got the directions off Lizzie and hurried out to her car. The schools were just finishing for the day and it took some time to get through the town centre traffic. She took the road to Dentons Cove, relieved that she'd been that way before when Tom had taken her to Susan Allsop's home. At least she had an idea where she was going, even though she hadn't been paying very much attention on the journey.

She sighed. She'd been more concerned about what had been happening between her and Tom to take notice of the scenery. Even though she'd only known him for a short time, she'd been aware of the attraction between them. Right from the beginning, Tom had made her feel things she had never felt before and it made her realise that she had never really loved Andrew. He had merely conformed to her view of the perfect mate but he had never aroused her passion, certainly never made her want him the way she wanted Tom. Tom might not be perfection, but he was perfect for *her*.

The thought was the last thing she needed. Hannah forced it from her mind as she drove along the road. She came to a bend and slowed down because from what Lizzie had told her, she must be nearing her destination. She rounded the bend and spotted several cars drawn up at the side of the road. There was a police car there and the officer came over when she pulled up.

'I'm Hannah Morris, one of the doctors from Bride's Bay Surgery.'

'Good to meet you, Doc. If you could park over there in that field, I'll take you across to meet the team.'

Hannah parked her car and followed him to where a group of people was gathered near the edge of the cliff. Susan Allsop was one of them and she came hurrying over to her.

'I'm so glad you're here, Hannah! It's one of our guests who's fallen, a man called Ian Lawson. I don't know how it happened. We always make it clear that everyone must stay away from the edge, don't we, Brian?'

'We do, but some folk won't be told,' Brian Allsop replied philosophically. A tall man with a bushy grey beard, he smiled at Hannah. 'The chap who's fallen doesn't take kindly to being given advice. He seems to think he knows better than everyone else does.'

'Oh, dear. That doesn't bode well,' Hannah replied, grimacing.

She looked round when a small man with bright red hair came over and introduce himself as Alan Parker, the leader of the search and rescue team. They shook hands before he led her to the cliff edge.

'He's stuck about halfway down on a ledge. One of our guys has been down to take a look at him and he's in a pretty bad way. His leg's busted and he's probably got concussion as well. To be frank, Hannah, we're not happy about moving him until you've seen him. We don't want to cause any more damage.'

'Of course,' Hannah agreed, her heart sinking at the thought of having to climb down the cliff. 'What do you want me to do?'

'If you're happy with the idea then we'll lower you down to the ledge. You'll be wearing a rope and a harness so you'll be quite safe. One of the team's down there, John Banks, and he'll help you.' Alan glanced at her shoes. 'I don't suppose you have anything else to wear apart from those heels, do you?'

'I'm afraid not.'

'I can lend you a pair of flat shoes,' Susan offered, overhearing what had been said. 'I keep a spare pair in the car in case we go somewhere muddy. We're about the same size, I imagine.'

'Thank you.' Hannah smiled at her. 'Obviously, I need to be better prepared in the future.'

Susan hurried off to fetch the shoes while Alan and one of the other men sorted out the harness. Fortunately, Hannah was wearing trousers so it was a simple matter to slip it on. Once the clasps had been fastened and checked, a rope was attached to the metal loop at the front. Susan had come back with the shoes by then and Hannah put them on. Then she was led to the edge of the cliff.

'It'll be easier if you go down backwards,' Alan explained. 'I don't know what you're like with heights but most folk find it a bit daunting to see nothing but sky in front of them.'

Hannah nodded, saving her breath for the descent. She knelt down and inched her way over the edge of the cliff, her heart pounding as she tried to find a foothold. She managed to jam her toe into a crack in the rocks and heaved a sigh of relief. At least she'd overcome the first hurdle!

It took her a good five minutes to reach the ledge and she was trembling by the time she got there. The injured man was lying on his side with John Banks crouched beside him. Hannah knelt down next to them, very conscious of the fact that inches away from them the land fell away in a sheer drop. It would be straight down into the sea if they weren't careful.

'How's he doing?' she asked, trying not to think about that.

'Not too good. His leg's in a right state and I've no idea what the rest of him's like.'

Hannah checked the man's leg, frowning when she discovered a nasty open fracture of the tibia.

'I see what you mean. That needs covering before infection sets in.'

She carried on with her examination, gently rotating the man's hips as a fall like this could result in a fracture to the pelvis. She grimaced when she found definite signs of instability. 'He's got a fractured pelvis. The main problem when that happens is the damage it can cause to the underlying organs, particularly the bladder. He'll need immediate surgery so getting him out of here is a priority. Is the helicopter on standby, do you know?'

'I'll check.'

Hannah continued her examination while the information was relayed. Although the patient was unconscious, it was impossible to say how serious his head injury was. A CT scan would reveal any underlying damage so that was another reason for getting him to hospital as quickly as possible.

'Alan's put in a request for the helicopter but they've been called to another incident,' John informed her finally. 'If they finish there before we're done, they'll fly over. Otherwise I'm afraid it's a trip by ambulance for him.'

'That's a shame but there's nothing we can do,' Hannah agreed. She set to work, covering the open fracture with a dressing before helping John fit an inflatable splint to the leg. Her next task was to stabilise his pelvis, which took rather longer. By the time she'd finished, the patient was coming round. Not surprisingly he seemed groggy and disorientated.

'I'm Hannah Morris and I'm a doctor,' she told him, laying a hand on his shoulder when he tried to sit up. 'You've had a nasty fall and you need to lie still.'

'I want to get up!' he exclaimed, giving her a hefty push.

Hannah reeled backwards, gasping when she felt herself tipping over the edge of the ledge. Fortunately, John managed to grab her harness and haul her back but she was shaking by the time she was upright again.

'Are you all right?' John asked in concern, and she drummed up a smile.

'Just about.' She turned to the injured man. 'I'm going to give you something for the pain. Then we'll see about getting you out of here. It will be easier for all of us if you do as you're told. Understand?'

He didn't reply, muttering something under his breath that she couldn't hear. Hannah ignored him as she drew up a shot of morphine and administered it. The sooner they were back at the top of the cliff the better.

It all took some time. Hannah offered to stay while a second member of the team was lowered down to help get the injured man onto a stretcher. Although the morphine had helped, it could need a second dose to deaden the pain and she wanted to be on hand. There was very little room with four of them crammed into such a small space but they finally got the patient secured and the order was given to raise him. Hannah kept close to the cliff face as bits of rock and other debris that had been dislodged by the stretcher began to tumble down. The stretcher was finally hauled over the top and she breathed a sigh of relief. Another couple of minutes and she'd be back on terra firma.

The thought had barely crossed her mind when she felt the ground beneath her start to sway. She let out a yelp of fear as she realised that the ledge itself was starting to give way. She scrabbled at the cliff face, trying to find hand—and foot-holes, but it was hopeless; a second later she was hanging, suspended in mid-air, with only the rope saving her from a long drop into the sea. She closed her eyes, feeling the fear rise up inside her, fear not for herself but for Charlie. Who would look after Charlie if anything happened to her?

Unbidden a picture came to mind and she bit her lip. Tom wouldn't do it. Why should he? And yet the thought lingered, a thought so ridiculous that she shouldn't have given it a moment's consideration: if she had to choose someone to look after her beloved son, she couldn't think of anyone better than Tom.

Tom arrived back at the surgery on time by the skin of his teeth. Only by rushing through the last couple of calls had he managed not to be late, and it wasn't a situation he enjoyed. It wasn't fair not to give every patient his full attention but he'd had no choice. He didn't want Hannah having to work late again tonight if he could help it.

He sighed as pushed open the door. Worrying about Hannah was becoming a habit. He hated to see her looking so tired and drawn. He'd over-heard her telling Emily that Charlie wasn't sleep-ing and could imagine how exhausted she must be. Lack of sleep on top of the pressure of work was enough to wear anyone out and he knew that he had to do something about it. The problem was what could he do when she kept refusing his help?

'Made it,' he declared, forcing himself not to go down the same old route. The reason why Han-nah wouldn't allow him to help her was because he was leaving. She didn't want to rely on him when there was no point. It would be different if he stayed, though, wouldn't it? Then he could persuade her to accept his help…and a whole lot more.

Heat poured through his veins and he breathed

in sharply to control the rush of desire that made him go weak. It was a moment before he realised that he'd missed what Lizzie had said. 'Sorry, what was that?'

'I said it's a good job you're back because Hannah's not here.'

'Where's she gone? I thought she was covering the antenatal clinic this afternoon,' Tom said, puzzled.

'She was. She did. But Jim Cairns phoned not long after it finished to say that someone had fallen off the cliffs between here and Dentons Cove,' Lizzie explained. 'The S and R team didn't have a doctor so they asked if you or Hannah could attend. I've no idea what time she'll be back.'

'I see.' Tom felt unease hit him as he glanced at his watch. Although Hannah hadn't been gone that long, he would feel better if he spoke to her. He came to a swift decision. 'I'll give her a call and see how it's going.'

'Would you? Thanks. I'd do it myself but people are already starting to arrive.'

Tom went out to the porch and called Hannah's mobile but there was no reply. That didn't mean much, of course; she could be too busy to answer or in a place where there was poor reception. There were areas all around Bride's Bay where it was impossible to make or receive mobile phone calls. He put his phone away and went to get ready for surgery, but all the time he was sorting things out he couldn't stop worrying about Hannah. The thought that she might be in danger wouldn't go away. He couldn't bear to think that something bad might happen to her. He couldn't bear it for any number of reasons, the main one being that imagining a world without Hannah in it was *impossible.*

Tom had just seen his last patient out when Lizzie came rushing into the room. By some minor miracle, it hadn't been as busy that night and he'd been able to cover Hannah's list as well as his own. He rose to his feet, his heart pounding because he could tell that something had happened.

'What is it? Is it Hannah?'

'Yes! Alan Parker's just phoned to say that she's been taken to hospital.' Lizzie's voice caught. 'Apparently, the ledge she was on gave way.'

'What! Did she fall? Is she badly injured?' Tom demanded.

'I don't know. The reception was so bad that I could barely hear what Alan was trying to tell me. All I know is that she's been taken to the hospital,' Lizzie explained.

'I'll get onto ED and find out what's going on,' Tom told her, reaching for the phone. He paused. 'What about Charlie? He needs to be picked up from nursery.'

'Emily had already offered to collect him if Hannah wasn't back so she's going to take him home with her.'

'Good. That's one less thing to worry about.'

Tom didn't waste any more time as he put through the call. He quickly explained who he was and why he was calling but was met with the usual stone wall: it was hospital policy not to give out information about a patient to anyone who wasn't a relative. He slammed down the phone and stormed towards the door. They'd have a far harder job telling him that to his face.

The drive to the hospital seemed to take forever. By the time he found somewhere to park his nerves were at breaking point. It didn't help that he kept picturing Hannah lying like a broken doll at the bottom of the cliff. Fear rose up inside him but he forced it down. Now wasn't the time to lose control, not when he needed to get past all the usual bureaucracy. He made his way to the reception desk.

'You have a patient here by the name of Hannah Morris. I'd like to see her.'

'And you are?'

This was the tricky bit. Tom knew that if he said he was a colleague he hadn't a hope of getting in to see her. He took a deep breath but the words seemed to flow so easily off his tongue that they didn't sound like a lie. Maybe that was because he wanted them to be true more than he'd ever wanted anything.

'I'm her partner, Tom Bradbury.'

# CHAPTER FIFTEEN

HANNAH was just leaving the treatment room when she saw Tom standing by the reception desk. She stopped dead, shocked to see him there where she'd least expected it.

'I'm her partner, Tom Bradbury.'

Her breath caught when she heard the emotion in his voice. No one hearing it could have misunderstood what he meant but it didn't make sense. Tom wasn't her partner, not in that sense…not in any sense. He was a free agent, a man who avoided commitment like the plague.

'Oh, right. I see. If you'd care to wait a moment, Mr Bradbury, I'll see what I can find out for you.'

The receptionist had obviously heard the same thing that she had done, Hannah realised giddily. She put her hand on the wall to steady herself as the room began to swim. What was going on? Why was Tom claiming to be something he wasn't? She had no idea and before she could work it out he glanced round and saw her.

'Hannah!'

There it was again, that wealth of emotions that ranged from fear to something she was afraid to put a name to. That couldn't be love she could hear in his voice; it simply couldn't! Her head was reeling as he hurried over to her so that she could only stand there and stare at him in silence.

'Are you all right? I couldn't believe it when Lizzie told me you'd been brought here...' He tailed off, his face chalk white, his eyes haunted. He looked like a man who had suffered some sort of terrible shock and Hannah did the only thing she could think of, the only thing that made any kind of sense. Opening her arms, she wrapped them around him and held him, feeling the shudder that passed through him as his arms closed around her.

'I was so scared,' he said hoarsely. 'So afraid that I might never see you again.'

'And that would have mattered to you?' she said softly.

'Yes.' He took her face between his hands. 'I can't bear to think of a world without you in it, Hannah. I don't even want to try.'

He kissed her then, his lips saying everything he couldn't bring himself to say, and Hannah felt a wave of happiness rise up inside her. Tom *loved* her. Maybe he hadn't said the actual words but she knew it was true, knew that it was time *she* admitted the truth. She smiled up at him with her heart in her eyes. 'You don't need to imagine it, Tom, because I'm not going anywhere...'

'Hannah! Thank heavens you're still here.'

Hannah swung round when she recognised Emily's voice. Fear rose up inside her when she saw that her friend was carrying Charlie. 'What's happened?' she demanded, hurrying over to them.

'Theo tried to carry Charlie upstairs and dropped him,' Emily explained. 'He fell down about three steps and banged his head on the newel post at the bottom.'

She turned Charlie round so that Hannah could

see the huge bruise on the his forehead. Hannah gasped in dismay as she lifted him out of Emily's arms. 'Oh, you poor little thing!'

'I am *so* sorry. I'd only gone to make them a drink and then I heard Charlie scream…'

Emily broke off and shuddered. Hannah could tell how awful she felt and despite her concern for her son knew that she couldn't let Emily torture herself this way.

'It was an accident,' she said firmly, rocking Charlie to and fro when he started to whimper. 'It wasn't your fault, Emily. It was just one of those things that happen.'

'But it was my fault! I know what a little monkey Theo can be and I should never have left him alone with Charlie,' Emily protested.

'You can't watch kids every second of the day. As Hannah said, it was an accident, Emily, and you aren't to blame.'

Tom added his own reassurances and Hannah felt a shiver run through her. If Emily had arrived a few seconds later she would have admitted to Tom how she felt but would it have been the right thing to do?

Maybe it had been an accident but if she'd been taking care of Charlie herself, it might never have happened. Guilt filled her at the thought that she had failed her son. How could she think of telling Tom that she loved him, with all that it entailed, when she should be concentrating on making sure that Charlie was safe?

Thoughts rushed through her head. She was barely aware of Emily leaving or the fact that Tom had gone to the desk and demanded that Charlie be seen immediately. She carried the baby into a cubicle, sitting down on the couch with him on her knee while the registrar checked him over. Although Charlie seemed alert and responsive, the registrar decided that he should have a CT scan. They were ushered to the radiology unit by one of the nursing staff and left there.

Charlie took a very dim view of all the machinery and kicked up a fuss but in the end the scan was done and they returned to A and E. The registrar was with another patient so they had to wait. Hannah turned to Tom, hoping that she could persuade him to leave. Quite frankly, she needed time on her own to come to terms with what had happened, not only to Charlie but between them.

'There's no knowing how long this will take so why don't you go on home? It seems pointless you hanging around here.'

'I'd like to make sure that Charlie's OK,' he said flatly, and she could tell from his tone that he'd seen through her ruse. Colour ran up her face but she met his gaze.

'It will be easier if you leave, Tom. I need to focus on Charlie, and I don't intend to let anything or anyone distract me.'

An expression of pain crossed his face as he stood up. 'If that's how you feel then of course I'll leave. Have you enough money for a taxi?'

She hadn't thought about that and bit her lip. A fine mother she was when she didn't even have the means to get her child home. Tom handed her some notes and she murmured her thanks, avoiding his eyes in case she weakened. She didn't want him to leave but what choice did she have? Charlie came first—he had to.

'If you need me then phone, Hannah. Promise?'

Tom bent and looked into her eyes and it was all she could do not to beg him to put his arms around her. The temptation to lean on him was so strong that she wasn't sure how she managed to resist but she did.

'Don't worry about us. We'll be fine, won't we, sweetheart?' She dropped a kiss on Charlie's cheek because it was easier to look at him than at Tom.

'Fine.' Tom straightened abruptly and she could tell from his stance that he was both physically and mentally drawing away from her. Her heart ached at the thought even though it was what she wanted. There wasn't room in her life for him and Charlie.

Tears welled to her eyes as she watched him leave. Whatever they could have had together was over. Tom wouldn't try to win her round and why should he now that he understood the situation? Few men would wish to play second fiddle to another man's child and Tom was no different from anyone else.

\* \* \*

Tom felt completely numb as he got into his car. It was as though every scrap of emotion had drained from his body, leaving him feeling like an empty shell. He drove out of the car park, automatically taking the road that led to Bride's Bay. Hannah didn't want him—that was what it boiled down to. She didn't want him in her life and he couldn't blame her in a way. He'd hardly set himself up as the perfect catch, had he? He'd banged on and on about not doing commitment, about not wanting to settle down; what sane woman would want him in her life, especially when she had a child to consider? Hannah had done the only thing she could do, the only *sensible* thing—she'd sent him packing and he should accept that and write it off to experience…

Only he couldn't! He couldn't just walk away and leave her to get on with her life when he loved her. He couldn't turn his back on Charlie either. Somehow the little tyke had wormed his way into his heart and he couldn't bear to think that he wouldn't be around to watch him growing up. He should never have allowed her to push him away!

Tom cursed roundly as he turned the car around and headed back to the hospital. He knew that Hannah wouldn't welcome him but hard luck. Maybe he wouldn't be able to talk her round but by heaven he was going to give it his best shot! He made his way into A and E, heading straight for the cubicles. Hannah gasped when he pushed aside the curtain and he could tell that she was nonplussed by his arrival. Good. Maybe he'd have the chance to state his side of the argument this time.

'I know what you're going to say, Hannah, so don't bother. Every word you uttered before is etched on my heart.' He pressed his hand to his chest in a gesture that would have seemed melodramatic any other time but now merely reflected how deeply he felt.

'In that case, why are you here?' she said acerbically, but he heard the quaver in her voice and knew that it was no easier for her than it was for him. The thought spurred him on.

'Because you're making a mistake. Oh, not about taking care of Charlie, obviously. He has to come first and I wouldn't want it any other way. But cutting me out of your life isn't what you really want, is it?' He smiled at her, hoping he looked more confident than he felt. Everything hinged on his ability to convince her that his feelings were genuine, that they would last a lifetime and beyond.

Once again the old doubts surfaced but he thrust them aside. This wasn't the time to waver; this was the time for action! 'You're doing it because you think it's the right thing to do, because you're afraid that I won't be able to handle the situation.'

'Charlie's father couldn't,' she shot back, but he saw the pain in her eyes and knew how much she was hurting so didn't take offence.

'I know he couldn't. More fool him for letting go of something so precious, is all I can say.'

He went over to the couch and knelt in front of her, placing his hand on Charlie's head. The baby was half-asleep but he smiled gummily at him and Tom felt his heart overflow with love.

He could hear the emotion in his voice when he continued but he didn't care. He loved this child as much as he would love his own children if he was lucky enough to have some one day.

'More fool him for letting go of you too, Hannah.' He lent forward and kissed her, his lips lingering for a single heartbeat before he drew back. He didn't intend to push his luck by being too forward. 'That's something I'll never do.'

'I thought you didn't do commitment? How did you put it? Ah, yes, you're genetically programmed to be unfaithful. Not exactly confidence inspiring, is it, Tom?' She stared back at him and he could tell that she was determined to hold out. He smiled inwardly. That was all right because he was just as determined.

'No, it isn't. It's not the least bit inspiring so I don't blame you if you're sceptical about my sincerity. What I will say is that I've never felt this way about anyone before. I want to be with you, Hannah, not just for today or for the next month or the next year even but forever. I want to share your life, yours and Charlie's lives, and I want you both to share mine.'

'It's easy to say that now but you could change your mind. Looking after a baby isn't easy and when you factor in the other problems…'

'I understand all that.' He could tell she was working herself up into an outright rebuttal and headed her off, afraid that if he didn't do so they'd be back to square one, with him out in the cold both physically and metaphorically speaking. 'I understand that Charlie will need treatment for his talipes and that it could be intensive at times too.' He shrugged. 'I'll cope. We'll cope. Together.' He cracked a smile, hoping to lighten the mood. 'Don't they say that things are better done in pairs? Tea for two. It takes two to tango…'

'We'd be three, though. You, me and *Charlie*. How does that support your theory?'

She was as sharp as a tack and she'd drawn blood but he'd be damned if he'd be put off. 'Three it is, then. The Three Musketeers against the world. Sounds good to me.'

'I know you mean well, Tom…'

'I do.' He cut her off, not giving a fig about politeness. 'I want what's best for you and Charlie, Hannah.'

'And what if I think it's better if you stay out of our lives?'

'Then I'll have to do what you want. If I can't persuade you to see sense then I'll abide by your wishes.' He stood up, his heart breaking because not even his best efforts were having an effect. 'I won't try to badger you into doing something you don't want to do. I love you too much for that. If you can't imagine a future with me, I'll have to accept it, no matter how hard it is.'

He turned to leave, defeat weighing him down. He had failed spectacularly, failed to win her back, and now he would have to suffer the consequences.

'Tom, wait.'

He stopped abruptly, praying that she wasn't going to apologise. He couldn't bear that, couldn't stand to hear her say she was sorry because she could never love him. Pain ripped through his guts so that it took every scrap of willpower to stand there like a condemned man waiting to hear his fate. 'Yes?'

'I can imagine a future with you. That's what scares me.'

It was the last thing he'd expected her to say. He spun round, his heart pounding as he stared at her. 'I don't understand.'

'It's simple. I can picture us growing old together and imagine the life we could have raising Charlie and any other children that may come along. But is it a pipe dream? Can it really happen or am I fooling myself into thinking that it can?' She sighed as she glanced at the baby. 'Charlie was rejected by his own father and I can't and won't take the chance of him being rejected again.'

'I would never, *ever* reject him.' He strode back into the cubicle and knelt in front of her. 'I'd never do that to any child and certainly not to this little fellow.' His voice broke because he wasn't used to dealing with all this emotion. 'I'd never do it to you, either, Hannah, because I love you too much.'

'Are you sure? Absolutely certain that you know what you're saying? It's a big commitment, Tom. It's not like buying a new car or changing jobs. It's for ever and ever and you need to be sure that you can handle that kind of scenario.' She bit her lip. 'I'd hate it if one day you came to regret it. I don't want us to become a burden to you.'

'You could never be that.'

He drew her into his arms, her and Charlie, and held them close, held them to his heart where they would always remain. All of a sudden all his doubts melted away and he knew—he just knew!—that he could do it. He could offer Hannah the happy-ever-after she deserved and mean it. Mean it with every fibre of his being, every tiny molecule that made him who he was. There wasn't a gene in his body that could make him change his mind about this.

He kissed her tenderly, hungrily, loving the way she kissed him back without reservation. That more than anything told him that she believed him and he made himself a promise right there and then that he would never do anything to betray her trust. It was only when the registrar appeared that they broke apart but even then he kept hold of her hand, needing the contact as much as he sensed she needed it too. They were in this together and would face whatever life threw at them side by side.

'It's good news,' the registrar informed them cheerfully. 'The scan's clear so you can take this little fellow home. If I were you I'd get a gate for the stairs until he's mastered the art of getting up and down them.'

'We'll do that.' Tom stood up, overwhelmed with relief as he shook the other man's hand. 'Thank you.'

'My pleasure.' The registrar smiled. 'I've not got kids myself but I can imagine that they must put you through the mill at times.'

'I expect they do,' Tom concurred, glancing at Hannah. 'But it's worth it.'

Hannah smiled, feeling her heart overflow with happiness. No matter how hard it was, Tom was going to stick around. He helped her to her feet after the registrar left, putting his arms around her and holding her so tightly that she couldn't contain the groan that slid from her lips.

'Darling, what is it?' he demanded in concern.

'A couple of badly bruised ribs, I'm afraid. You need to treat me like the most delicate china,' she told him with a grin.

'That won't be difficult.' He dropped a kiss on her nose then gently put his arm around her waist. 'Is that better?'

'Much. Thank you.' She smiled into his eyes, loving the way they darkened with desire. Her heart was racing as he led her and Charlie from the cubicle. He stopped when they reached the main doors.

'You two wait here while I fetch the car.'

'I can manage to walk to the car,' she protested, laughing at him.

'I'm sure you can, but I don't want you pushing yourself. Apart from those bruised ribs, you've had a couple of nasty shocks today and you need to take things easy.'

Hannah nodded. Just thinking about those terrible minutes when she'd been left dangling at the end of that rope made her feel sick, and then there was Charlie's accident... She shuddered and Tom's face darkened as he led her over to a chair and sat her down.

'Stay here. I just need to pop over to Jim Cairns's garage to borrow a baby seat for Charlie. It'll only take me a couple of minutes. OK?'

'Fine. We'll be right here, Tom, waiting for you.'

An expression of joy crossed his face as he bent and kissed her. 'I love you, Hannah. So much.'

'I love you too,' she whispered, meaning it with all her heart.

Tom kissed her again then hurried out of the door. Charlie was fast asleep, worn out by the events of the day, so she closed her eyes, letting the emotions wash over her. Happiness was the main one, of course, although she had to admit that there was uncertainty too. Was she being overly optimistic by thinking that Tom had conquered his fears about commitment? Oh, she didn't doubt that he loved her—she could tell that he did from the way he looked at her. But would the time ever come when he'd feel ready for marriage? She had no idea but she needed to face the fact that Tom might never be ready to take that final step.

Tom parked outside the main doors and took a deep breath. Everything had happened so fast that his head was spinning. Hannah loved him—he could barely take it in. And yet in a funny way it didn't seem strange that she should. After all, he loved her, didn't he?

His heart sang with happiness at the thought. He felt like leaping out of the car and shouting it out loud so everyone could hear but he didn't think it would go down too well with the security guard who was heading towards him to tell him to move his car. Not even a declaration of love would permit him to park illegally!

He jumped out of the car, ignoring the man's shout as he hurried inside. Hannah was sitting where he'd left her and his heart swelled that bit more. She was so precious to him that he wanted to sweep her into his arms and never let her go. This time it was forever.

He helped her to her feet, his arm snaking

around her waist as they went out to the car. There was an envelope under the wiper—undoubtedly a parking ticket—but he tossed it into the back with barely a glance. He couldn't care less if he was given a dozen tickets so long as Hannah wasn't inconvenienced!

The drove back to Bride's Bay in silence. Tom guessed that she had a lot to think about, as he did. He drew up outside her house, wondering where they went from here. It had been different at the hospital. He'd been propelled by a sense of urgency then, but now that it had passed he wasn't sure what happened next. Should he ask her if he could come in so they could talk or would it be better if he left it until tomorrow?

'I need to get Charlie to bed,' she said, glancing at him.

'Do you want me to go?' he asked, not wanting to push her any more than he already had.

'No. Unless you want to, of course.'

'I don't.' He kissed her on the cheek then opened the car door. 'I'll get Charlie out for you.'

He opened the rear door and lifted Charlie out of his seat, thinking how right it felt to do such a thing. This was where he belonged. 'How about I take Charlie up and give him his bath?'

'You don't have to do that, Tom,' she protested, and he smiled.

'I know, but I'd really like to—if you trust me enough, of course.'

'Of course I trust you,' she said immediately, and his smile widened. Hannah trusted him with her precious child and that meant the world to him. He bent and kissed her on the cheek.

'Thank you. It's good to hear you say that.' He stood up and turned the baby round to face him. 'OK, it's you and me from here on, tiger. Be gentle with me, won't you? I'm a complete novice at this!'

Charlie chuckled as he made a grab for his nose and Tom laughed. He carried the baby inside and up to the bathroom and turned on the taps, feeling a sense of peace fill him. Maybe there were still some issues that he and Hannah needed to sort out, but there was nothing they couldn't deal with so long as they did it together. They loved each other and nothing was going to keep them apart from now on.

* * *

Hannah stripped off her filthy clothes and tossed them into the hamper. Taking her dressing gown out of the wardrobe, she pulled it on and stepped in front of the mirror. She looked a mess, she decided. Her hair was in tangles and there was a smudge of dirt on her cheek, but it seemed too much of an effort to take a shower. She wiped off the worst of the dirt then ran a brush through her hair and headed downstairs. Tom would have finished bathing Charlie soon and she would need to get him ready for bed, or rather ready to begin their nightly routine. She sighed. Please heaven Charlie wouldn't kick up his usual fuss tonight of all nights.

She went into the sitting room and sat down on the sofa, closing her eyes as she rested her head against the cushions. It had been a long day and she was worn out after everything that had happened. She must have drifted off to sleep because the next thing she knew Tom was gently waking her.

'I've made you some tea and sandwiches,' he told her, pointing to the tray.

'What about Charlie?' she said, quickly rousing herself.

'Fast asleep. I just popped him in his cot and that was it.'

'I should have told you that he needed his boots back on,' she said worriedly, scrambling to her feet.

'It's all sorted.' Tom gently pushed her back down onto the cushions. 'I popped them back on before I put him in his cot.'

'Really?' Hannah gasped. 'And he didn't object?'

'I think he was too tired to bother.' He sat down and grinned at her. 'We played a rather soggy game of submarines while he was in the bath and I think that wore him out. I'm afraid the floor's a bit of a mess, although it should dry eventually.'

'Don't worry about the floor! The fact that you managed to settle him at all is a minor miracle. He hates having his boots back on after I've bathed him. You'll have to give me a few tips.'

'It was probably the novelty factor. Being bathed by me distracted him.'

'Well, whatever it was I owe you a vote of thanks. There's nothing more stressful than having to do something that you know is going to upset your child.'

Tears sprang to her eyes and she heard Tom sigh. 'You've had a lot to contend with recently, Hannah.'

'It's no worse for me than it is for any other working mum,' she countered, not wanting him to think that she was looking for sympathy.

'I'd dispute that if I didn't suspect it could start us arguing,' he teased, and she laughed.

'We won't argue.'

'No?'

'No.' She took a quick breath. 'I don't want to argue with you, Tom. It's the last thing I want to do.'

'Me too. Or should that be neither?' He took hold of her hands. 'I love you, Hannah.'

'And I love you too.' She smiled at him. 'See? We're in total agreement.'

He laughed and pulled Hannah closer. 'So it appears.'

'And you're sure about what you're doing?' She bit her lip when she heard the uncertainty in her voice. Tom obviously heard it too because he gripped her hands even tighter.

'I am sure. One hundred per cent certain, in fact. I love you, Hannah, and I want to spend my life with you. I want to be there whenever you need me and be a father to Charlie, too.'

'And you don't think you'll change your mind?' she said, needing all the reassurance he could give her.

'I know I won't. This is it. You are what's been missing from my life.' He kissed her on the mouth then drew back. 'Please believe me. I don't want you torturing yourself with doubts and spoiling what we have. I'm in this for the long haul. For ever.'

'Oh, Tom!'

Hannah put her arms around him and hugged him. There wasn't a doubt in her mind that he was sincere. Tom loved her and he would be there for her every single day and every night too. Maybe he hadn't mentioned marriage but it no longer seemed important. They didn't need a piece of paper to confirm their love; they just needed each other. And Charlie, of course, because he was part of this too.

They made love right there on the sofa and it was even more wonderful than before. Maybe it was the fact that they had admitted their feelings at last but they seemed to reach new heights. Hannah gave herself up to the glory of their love-making, sure that she had made the right decision. Maybe she hadn't planned on falling in love so soon but it didn't matter. Tom loved her and she loved him, and they were going to spend their lives together. Everything had worked out perfectly.

\* \* \* \* \*

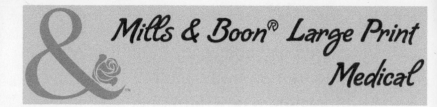

# Mills & Boon® Large Print Medical

0413 LP 1P Medical